PENGUIN B

THE MOON I

Born in Salinas, California, in 1902, JOHN STEINBECK grew up in a fertile agricultural valley about twenty-five miles from the Pacific Coast—and both valley and coast would serve as settings for some of his best fiction. In 1919 he went to Stanford University, where he intermittently enrolled in literature and writing courses until he left in 1925 without taking a degree. During the next five years he supported himself as a laborer and journalist in New York City and then as a caretaker for a Lake Tahoe estate, all the time working on his first novel, *Cup of Gold* (1929). After marriage and a move to Pacific Grove, he published two California fictions, *The Pastures of Heaven* (1932) and *To a God Unknown* (1933), and worked on short stories later collected in *The Long Valley* (1938). Popular success and financial security came only with *Tortilla Flat* (1935), stories about Monterey's paisanos. A ceaseless experimenter throughout his career, Steinbeck changed courses regularly. Three powerful novels of the late 1930s focused on the California laboring class: *In Dubious Battle* (1936), *Of Mice and Men* (1937), and the book considered by many his finest, *The Grapes of Wrath* (1939). Early in the 1940s, Steinbeck became a filmmaker with *The Forgotten Village* (1941) and a serious student of marine biology with *Sea of Cortez*. He devoted his services to the war, writing *Bombs Away* (1942) and the controversial play-novelette *The Moon Is Down* (1942). *Cannery Row* (1945), *The Wayward Bus* (1947), *The Pearl* (1947), *A Russian Journal* (1948), another experimental drama, *Burning Bright* (1950), and *The Log from the* Sea of Cortez (1951) preceded publication of the monumental *East of Eden* (1952), an ambitious saga of the Salinas Valley and his own family's history. The last decades of his life were spent in New York City and Sag Harbor with his third wife, with whom he traveled widely. Later books include *Sweet Thursday* (1954), *The Short Reign of Pippin IV: A Fabrication* (1957), *Once There Was a War* (1958), *The Winter of Our Discontent* (1961), *Travels with Charley in Search of America* (1962), *America and Americans* (1966), and the posthumously published *Journal of a Novel: The* East of Eden *Letters* (1969), *Viva Zapata!* (1975), *The Acts of King Arthur and His Noble Knights* (1976), and *Working Days: The Journals of* The Grapes of Wrath (1989). He died in 1968, having won a Nobel Prize in 1962.

BY JOHN STEINBECK

FICTION

Cup of Gold	The Moon Is Down
The Pastures of Heaven	Cannery Row
To a God Unknown	The Wayward Bus
Tortilla Flat	The Pearl
In Dubious Battle	Burning Bright
Saint Katy the Virgin	East of Eden
Of Mice and Men	Sweet Thursday
The Red Pony	The Winter of Our Discontent
The Long Valley	The Short Reign of Pippin IV

The Grapes of Wrath
Las uvas de la ira (Spanish-language edition of *The Grapes of Wrath*)
The Acts of King Arthur and His Noble Knights

NONFICTION

Sea of Cortez: A Leisurely Journal of Travel and Research
(in collaboration with Edward F. Ricketts)
Bombs Away: The Story of a Bomber Team
A Russian Journal *(with pictures by Robert Capa)*
The Log from the *Sea of Cortez*
Once There Was a War
Travels with Charley in Search of America
America and Americans
Journal of a Novel: The *East of Eden* Letters
Working Days: The Journals of *The Grapes of Wrath*

PLAYS

Of Mice and Men
The Moon Is Down

COLLECTIONS

The Portable Steinbeck
The Short Novels of John Steinbeck
Steinbeck: A Life in Letters

OTHER WORKS

The Forgotten Village (documentary)
Zapata (includes the screenplay of *Viva Zapata!*)

CRITICAL LIBRARY EDITION

The Grapes of Wrath (edited by Peter Lisca)

THE
Moon is Down

PLAY
IN TWO PARTS

By John Steinbeck

PENGUIN BOOKS

PENGUIN BOOKS

Published by the Penguin Group
Penguin Group (USA) Inc., 375 Hudson Street, New York, New York 10014, U.S.A.
Penguin Group (Canada), 90 Eglinton Avenue East, Suite 700, Toronto,
Ontario, Canada M4P 2Y3 (a division of Pearson Penguin Canada Inc.)
Penguin Books Ltd, 80 Strand, London WC2R 0RL, England
Penguin Ireland, 25 St Stephen's Green, Dublin 2, Ireland
(a division of Penguin Books Ltd)
Penguin Group (Australia), 250 Camberwell Road, Camberwell, Victoria 3124,
Australia (a division of Pearson Australia Group Pty Ltd)
Penguin Books India Pvt Ltd, 11 Community Centre, Panchsheel Park,
New Delhi – 110 017, India
Penguin Group (NZ), 67 Apollo Drive, Rosedale, North Shore 0632,
New Zealand (a division of Pearson New Zealand Ltd)
Penguin Books (South Africa) (Pty) Ltd, 24 Sturdee Avenue,
Rosebank, Johannesburg 2196, South Africa
Penguin Books Ltd, Registered Offices: 80 Strand, London WC2R 0RL, England

First published in the United States of America by The Viking Press 1942
Published in Penguin Books 2009

1 3 5 7 9 10 8 6 4 2

ISBN 978-0-14-311719-3

Printed in the United States of America

Following is a copy of the original program:

MARTIN BECK THEATRE

BEGINNING TUESDAY, APRIL 7, 1942

OSCAR SERLIN

PRESENTS

JOHN STEINBECK'S

THE MOON IS DOWN

WITH

OTTO KRUGER　　　　　　RALPH MORGAN

DIRECTED BY CHESTER ERSKIN
PRODUCTION DESIGNED BY HOWARD BAY

CAST

(IN ORDER OF APPEARANGE)

DR. WINTER	Whitford Kane
JOSEPH	Joseph Sweeney
SERGEANT	Edwin Gordon
CAPTAIN BENTICK	John D. Seymour
MAYOR ORDEN	Ralph Morgan
MADAME ORDEN	Leona Powers
CORPORAL	Charles Gordon
COLONEL LANSER	Otto Kruger
GEORGE CORELL	E. J. Ballantine
ANNIE	Jane Seymour
SOLDIER	Kermit Kegley
MAJOR HUNTER	Russell Collins
LIEUTENANT PRACKLE	Carl Gose
CAPTAIN LOFT	Alan Hewitt
LIEUTENANT TONDER	William Eythe
SOLDIER	Victor Thorley
MOLLY MORDEN	Maria Palmer
ALEX MORDEN	Philip Foster
WILL ANDERS	George Keane
TOM ANDERS	LYLE BETTGER

PRODUCTION STAGE MANAGER, B. D. KRANZ

The action of the play occurs in a small mining town.
The time is the present.

PART I

The drawing-room of the Mayor's house.

SCENE I. Morning.

SCENE II. A few days later.

SCENE III. Two days later.

SCENE IV. That evening.

INTERMISSION

PART II

SCENE I. The drawing-room of the Mayor's house.
Three months later.

SCENE II. The living-room of Molly Morden's house.
The following evening.

SCENE III. The drawing-room. Two weeks later.

SCENE IV. The same. Half an hour later.

PART ONE

SCENE I

SCENE: *The drawing-room of the tiny palace of the* MAYOR *of a small mining town. The room is poor, but has about it a certain official grandeur; tarnished gold chairs with worn tapestry seats and backs, and the slight stuffiness of all official rooms. In the downstage R. wall is a fireplace with coal grate and a mantel of white marble on which there is a large porcelain clock, and behind it a dark frame filled with miniature pictures. Upstage two large windows, and up L., glass-paned doors to vestibule and stairs leading to the upper floor. Down L., a door which it will appear leads to the* MAYOR'S *bedroom. Upstage R., a door which apparently leads to the dining-room, kitchen and stairways in the upper part of the house. The grandeur of the room is carried out with completely useless but very beautiful bric-a-brac on mantel and on tables, and whatever lamps are necessary to light the scene. Altogether it is a warm room which, trying to be stiff and official, has from use become rather comfortable and pleasant. A small coal fire burns in the grate. A brass coal-scuttle stands on the hearth. An upholstered arm-chair stands near the fireplace. A chess game on a small table stands between the arm-chair and a side-chair which faces the arm-chair. In the center of the room is a large sofa with a small table at each end. The* MAYOR'S *desk and chair stand against the L. wall upstage of his bedroom door. On this wall hang three gold-framed paintings. R. of the vestibule doors is a large grandfather's clock. In the window alcove is an*

*elaborate table with a side-chair at its downstage side.
In this alcove, too, is a gold painted pedestal on which
stands an elaborate silver-leaf vase holder with a glass
vase filled with ferns. Side-chairs are L. of vestibule doors
and down L. facing the sofa. Wall L. of dining-room door
carries a large gold-framed painting. Below it stands a
console table. R. wall below dining-room door carries two
small gold-framed pictures. All the walls except the R.
one are covered with drapes of a dark red and gold figure.
A pleasant warm light comes into the room from the
outside.*

As the curtain rises, DR. WINTER, *bearded, simple and be-
nign, is sitting on the sofa. He is the town historian and
physician, and is dressed in a dark suit and very white
linen, but his shoes are heavy and thick-soled. He sits
rolling his thumbs over and over in his lap.*

JOSEPH, *the serving man of the* MAYOR, *goes about
straightening furniture, doing little things that by no
means need to be done, and occasionally looking at*
WINTER.

WINTER. [*Looking up from his thumbs.*] Eleven o'clock?
JOSEPH. [*Abstractedly carrying ash-tray from desk to
end table L. of sofa.*] Yes, sir, the note said eleven.
WINTER. [*Half-humorously.*] You read the note, Joseph?
JOSEPH. [*Ignoring the humor, carrying side-chair from
L.C. to L. of table U.C.*] No, sir. His Excellency read the
note to me.
WINTER. He always asks me to come when there's trouble.

[JOSEPH *moves about the room, straightening furniture
he has already straightened. He moves side-chair R.C.
to R. end of table U.C.*]

JOSEPH. Yes, sir.

WINTER. [*Amusingly.*] Eleven o'clock. [*He glances at watch he has taken from his pocket.*] And they'll be here, too. [*Pause.*] A time-minded people, Joseph.

JOSEPH. [*Not listening.*] Yes, sir.

WINTER. A time-minded people.

JOSEPH. Yes, sir.

WINTER. They hurry to their destiny as though it wouldn't wait.

JOSEPH. [*Obviously not listening.*] Quite right, sir.

WINTER. [*Rolling his thumbs rapidly and watching* JO-SEPH *discipline the table R. of sofa.*] What's the Mayor doing?

JOSEPH. Dressing to receive the Colonel, sir.

WINTER. [*In mock concern.*] And you aren't helping him? He'll be badly dressed by himself.

JOSEPH. [*Stuffily, crossing to mantel for small ornament which he places on table R. of sofa.*] Madame is helping him. Madame wants him to look his best. She is trimming the hair out of his ears. He won't let me do it. He says it tickles.

WINTER. Of course it tickles.

JOSEPH. [*Stuffily.*] Madame insists.

WINTER. [*Rises and crosses to mantel, lighting pipe. As he leaves sofa,* JOSEPH *straightens the pillows on it.*] We're so wonderful. Our country is invaded and Madame is holding the Mayor by the neck and trimming the hair from his ears.

JOSEPH. [*Sternly, crosses to table U.C., arranging chairs around table R. to L.*] He was getting shaggy, sir. His eyebrows, too. His Excellency is even more upset about having his eyebrows trimmed than his ears. He says that hurts.

WINTER. It does.

JOSEPH. She wants him to look his best. [JOSEPH *at L. end of table turns sharply to look at* WINTER.]

WINTER. [*Looking at clock.*] They're early. Let them in, Joseph.

[JOSEPH *goes into vestibule. The front door is heard opening. A* SOLDIER *steps in, dressed in a long coat, helmeted and carrying over his arm a submachine gun. He glances quickly about and then steps aside.* CAPTAIN BENTICK *enters and stands in the doorway.*]

NOTE *On Uniforms.* Throughout, the uniforms of both soldiers and officers are plain as possible. Rank can be indicated by small colored tabs at the collar, but little else. *Helmets* should be a variation on any obvious shape which will identify these as being soldiers of any known nation.

BENTICK. [*Looking at* WINTER. BENTICK *is a slightly overdrawn picture of an English gentleman. He has a slouch. His face is red, long nose, but rather pleasant, and he seems as unhappy in his uniform as most British General Officers are.* JOSEPH *follows* BENTICK *in and stands at door.*] Are you Mayor Orden?
WINTER. No. No, I am not.
BENTICK. You are an official?
WINTER. [*Coming toward him.*] I'm the town doctor. I'm a friend of the Mayor.
BENTICK. [*Crossing to him.*] Where is Mayor Orden?

[JOSEPH *crosses D.L. to watch.*]

WINTER. Dressing to receive you, sir. You *are* the Colonel?
BENTICK. [*Almost embarrassedly.*] I am Captain Bentick. [*He bows and* WINTER *bows slightly back to him.* BENTICK *continues, as though a little embarrassed at what he has to say.*] We search for weapons before the Commanding Officer enters a room. We mean no disrespect, sir. [*Calling to* SERGEANT.] Sergeant . . .

[SERGEANT *moves quickly to* JOSEPH *and runs his hands over his pockets.*]

SERGEANT. Nothing, sir.
BENTICK. [*To* WINTER.] I hope you will pardon us.

[SERGEANT *approaches* WINTER, *pats his pockets.*]

SERGEANT. Nothing, sir. [*He then crosses to fireplace, examines it, then goes to door R. Looks out.*]

[JOSEPH *watches* SERGEANT *and crosses to R. of clock.*]

BENTICK. [*He takes a card from his pocket, reads it and says.*] I believe there are some firearms here.
WINTER. You are thorough.

[SERGEANT *crosses to clock U.L., opens pendulum door and looks inside.*]

BENTICK. [*Crossing to fireplace.*] Yes, we are. We wouldn't have been so successful if we weren't.
WINTER. Do you know where every gun in the town is?
BENTICK. Nearly all, I guess. We had our people working here for quite a long time.

[SERGEANT *crosses to* MAYOR'S *desk and looks in drawers.*]

WINTER. Working here? Who?

[SERGEANT *crosses R. above sofa to door R. and exits.*]

BENTICK. Well, the work is done now. It's bound to come out. The man in charge here is named Corell.

[JOSEPH *follows* SERGEANT *to door R. Stops to listen for a moment, then exits after* SERGEANT.]

WINTER. [*Unbelieving.*] George Corell?

BENTICK. Yes.

WINTER. I don't believe it. I can't believe it. Why, George had dinner with me on Friday. Why, I've played chess with George night after night. You must be wrong. Why, he gave the big shooting match in the hills this morning —gave the prizes—

BENTICK. [*Crossing to door R.*] Yes—that was clever— there wasn't a soldier in town. [*He exits R.*]

WINTER. [*Crossing to fireplace.*] George Corell—

[*The door on the L. opens and* MAYOR ORDEN *enters. He is digging his right ear with his little finger. He is a fine-looking man of about sixty-five and he seems a little too common and too simple for the official morning coat he wears and the gold chain of office around his neck. His hair has been fiercely brushed, but already a few hairs are struggling to be free. He has dignity and warmth. Behind him* MADAME ORDEN *enters. She is small and wrinkled and fierce, and very proprietary. She considers that she created this man, and ever since he has been trying to get out of hand. She watches him constantly as the lady shower of a prize dog watches her entry at a dog show. She comes up beside the* MAYOR, *takes his hand and pulls his finger out of his ear and gently puts his hand to his side, the way she would take a baby's thumb from his mouth.*]

MADAME. I don't believe for a moment it hurts that much. [*She turns to* WINTER.] He won't let me fix his eyebrows.

MAYOR. It hurts.

MADAME. Very well, if you want to look like that. [*She sees* BENTICK *as he enters R. and crosses C. to sofa. She crosses to meet him.*] Oh! The Colonel!

[SERGEANT *enters after* BENTICK, *crosses U.L.C.* JOSEPH *follows* SERGEANT *on. Crosses U.R.*]

BENTICK. No, Ma'am . . . I am only preparing for the Colonel. Sergeant! [SERGEANT *comes quickly to* MAYOR *and runs his hands over his pockets.*] Excuse him, sir . . . it's the regulations. [SERGEANT *moves toward* MADAME, *but* BENTICK *stops him. She crosses to R. of* BENTICK. *He glances at card in his hand again.*] Your Excellency, I think you have firearms here. Two items, I believe.

MAYOR. [*Bewildered.*] Firearms! Guns, you mean? Yes, I have a shotgun and a sporting rifle.

BENTICK. Where are these guns, your Excellency?

MAYOR. [*Rubs his cheek and tries to think.*] Why, I think— [*He turns to* MADAME.]—Aren't they in the back of that cabinet in the bedroom, with the walking sticks?

MADAME. I don't know why you insist on keeping them in the bedroom. You never use them.

BENTICK. Sergeant. [SERGEANT *quickly goes offstage to bedroom.* MADAME *follows him off.*] It's an unpleasant duty. I'm sorry.

MAYOR. [*Deprecatingly.*] You know I don't hunt very much any more. I always think I'm going to, and then the season opens and I don't get out. I guess I don't take the pleasure in it I used to.

[SERGEANT *re-enters, carrying a double-barrelled shot-gun and a rather nice sporting rifle with a shoulder strap. He exits into vestibule.* MADAME *enters from bedroom after* SERGEANT.]

BENTICK. Thank you, your Excellency. [*Crossing to her.*] Thank you, Madame. [*He turns and bows slightly to* WINTER.] Thank you, Doctor. Colonel Lanser will be here directly. Good morning!

MAYOR. Good morning.

[BENTICK *exits by front door. Front door closes.*]

MADAME. [*Crossing U.C.*] For a moment I thought he was the Colonel.

[MAYOR *crosses L. to desk.*]

WINTER. [*Sardonically, crossing to sofa, sits.*] No, he is just protecting the Colonel.

MADAME. [*Thinking.*] I wonder how many officers will come? [*She looks over at* JOSEPH *and sees that he is shamelessly eavesdropping. She shakes her head at him and frowns and he exits R. She moves chess-table to L. of arm-chair.*] I don't know whether it would be correct to offer them tea or a glass of wine. It is so difficult to plan, when you don't know.

WINTER. [*Shakes his head and smiles and says in mock seriousness.*] It's been so long since we've been invaded, or invaded anyone else. I just don't know what's correct.

MAYOR. We won't offer them anything. I don't think the people would like it. *I* don't want to drink wine with them. [*Sits desk chair.*]

MADAME. [*Appealing to* WINTER.] Didn't people in the old days . . . leaders, that is . . . compliment each other . . . take a glass of wine—?

WINTER. [*Nodding.*] Yes, they did. Rulers used to play at war the way Englishmen play at hunting. When the fox was dead, they got together at a hunt breakfast. The Mayor is right, Madame. The town wouldn't want him to drink wine with the invader.

MADAME. [*Acidly, as she takes ornament* JOSEPH *set on table R. of sofa, back to mantel.*] They are all down listening to the music. Annie told me they were. Why shouldn't we keep proper decencies alive?

[*During her speech the* MAYOR *has appeared to be coming out of a dream. He looks steadily at* MADAME *and then says sharply.*]

MAYOR. [*Rises, crosses L.C.*] Madame, I think with your permission we will not have wine! [*She crosses to R. of sofa.*] The people are confused. We have lived at peace so long they don't quite believe in war. Six town boys were murdered this morning. We will have no hunt breakfast. The people do not fight wars for sport.

MADAME. [*In disbelief, crossing in above sofa.*] Murdered?

MAYOR. [*Bitterly.*] Our twelve soldiers were at the shooting match in the hills. They saw the parachutes and they came back. At the bend in the road by Toller's farm the machine guns opened on them and six were killed.

MADAME. [*Excitedly, crossing to him.*] Which ones were killed? Annie's sister's boy was there.

MAYOR. I don't know which ones were killed. [*He looks at WINTER.*] I don't even know how many soldiers are here. [*Crossing to sofa, sits L. of WINTER.*] . . . Do you know how many men the invader has?

WINTER. [*Shrugging.*] Not many, I think. Not over two hundred and fifty. But all with those little machine guns.

MAYOR. Have you heard anything about the rest of the country? Here there were parachutes, a little transport. It happened so quickly. [WINTER *raises his shoulders and drops them. The* MAYOR *says, rather hopelessly.*] Was there no resistance anywhere?

[WINTER *again shrugs his shoulders.*]

WINTER. I don't know. The wires are cut. There is no news.

MAYOR. And our soldiers . . . ?

WINTER. I don't know.

JOSEPH. [*Enters from R., crosses D. to sofa.*] I heard . . . that is, Annie heard . . . six of our men were killed by the machine guns. Annie heard three were wounded and captured.

MAYOR. But there were twelve.

JOSEPH. Annie heard three escaped.

MAYOR. [*Sharply.*] Which ones escaped?

JOSEPH. I don't know, sir. Annie didn't hear.

MADAME. [*Crossing R. to arm-chair.*] Joseph, when they come, don't stay in the room all the time. Stay close to your bell. We might want something. [*He starts for door.* MAYOR *rises, crosses to desk.* MADAME *looks at* JO-SEPH *critically.*] And put on your other coat, Joseph . . . [*He stops.*] . . . the one with the buttons. [*She sits arm-chair.* JOSEPH *starts again. Again she inspects* JOSEPH.] Joseph, when you finish what you are told to do, go out of the room. It makes a bad impression when you just stand around listening. It's provincial.

JOSEPH. Yes, Madame. [*He starts again for door.*]

MADAME. We won't serve wine, Joseph. [*He stops.*] But you might have some cigarettes handy . . . in that lit-tle silver conserve box. [*He starts.*] When you light the Colonel's cigarette, don't strike the match on your shoe. Strike it on the match-box.

JOSEPH. [*Coming to her L.*] Yes, Madame. They won't strike on the shoe, Madame. They are safety matches.

MADAME. Well, strike them on the box, then.

[WINTER *takes out his watch.*]

JOSEPH. Yes, Madame. [*He exits R.*]

MADAME. And don't forget His Excellency's coffee. [*She rises and exits R.*]

[MAYOR, *unbuttoning his coat, takes out his big gold watch, crosses to sofa.*]

WINTER. What time have you now?

MAYOR. Five of eleven.

[*They place their watches back in pockets.*]

WINTER. Do you want me to go?
MAYOR. [*A little startled.*] Oh, no, please stay. I'm nervous. I need you to stay.
WINTER. [*Rises, crosses to fireplace.*] You always send for me when there's trouble.

[*Marching feet can be heard approaching the house.*]

MAYOR. [*Chuckling.*] Yes, I do, don't I?
MADAME. [*Enters from R., excitedly, crosses to windows.* MAYOR *rises, crosses to desk.*] Here they come. I hope not too many try to crowd in here at once. It isn't a very big room. [MADAME *crosses L. to* MAYOR.]

[JOSEPH *enters from R. buttoning his coat, hurrying to the vestibule, exits U.L.*]

WINTER. [*Sardonically.*] Madame would prefer the hall of mirrors at Versailles?
MADAME. [*Pinching her lips, looking about.*] It's a very small room.

[*Outside is heard the command "Company halt!" The marching stops. A knock on the outside door is heard.*]

CORPORAL. [*Offstage.*] Colonel Lanser's compliments. . . . Colonel Lanser requests an audience with His Excellency. [*The helmeted* CORPORAL *steps inside, looks quickly about and then stands aside, front of clock U.L.C.*]

[*A second helmeted* FIGURE *steps into the room, his rank showing only on his shoulder. He, too, looks quickly about. The* COLONEL *is a middle-aged man, gray and hard and tired-looking. He has the square shoulders of a soldier, but his eyes lack the blank wall of a soldier's man.*]

COLONEL LANSER. [*After taking off his helmet, with a quick bow.*] Your Excellency. [*Bows to* MADAME.] Madame . . . [LANSER *looks questioningly at* WINTER.]

MAYOR. [*Fingering his chain of office.*] This is Dr. Winter.

LANSER. [*Courteously.*] An official?

MAYOR. A doctor, sir, and the local historian.

LANSER. [*Bows slightly, crossing to C.*] Dr. Winter. I do not mean to be impertinent, this will be a page in your history, perhaps.

WINTER. [*Smiling.*] Many pages, perhaps.

[GEORGE CORELL *enters quickly, places his coat and hat on chair U.L. corner, steps down to R. of* MAYOR. JOSEPH *follows* CORELL *on, closes doors and exits R.*]

LANSER. [*Turning slightly toward his companion.*] I think you know Mr. Corell! [*Crosses U.R. above sofa.*]

MAYOR. George Corell? Of course we know him. How are you, George?

CORELL. Good morning, sir. There are changes this morning.

WINTER. [*Cutting in.*] Your Excellency—I think you should know this. Our friend, George Corell, is a traitor.

MAYOR. What do you mean, a traitor?

[LANSER *crosses to table U.C., places helmet on table.*]

WINTER [*Crossing to arm-chair R.—sits.*] He prepared for this invasion. He sent our troops into the hills so they would be out of the way. He listed every firearm in the town. God knows what else he has done. . . .

CORELL. [*Crossing to* WINTER.] Doctor, you don't understand. This thing was bound to come. It's a good thing. You don't understand it yet, but when you do, you will thank me. The democracy was rotten and inefficient. Things will be better now. Believe me. [*Almost fanatic in his belief.*] When you understand the new order you will know I am right.

MAYOR. [*As though he had not heard the argument, turns to* MADAME.] George Corell—a traitor—?

CORELL. [*Impatiently, crossing to front of sofa.*] I work for what I believe in. That's an honorable thing.

MAYOR. [*Crossing to* CORELL.] This isn't true—George — [*Almost pleading.*] George—you've sat at my table —on Madame's right—we've played chess together. This isn't true, George—?

CORELL. [*Sits sofa.*] I work for what I believe in. You will agree with me when you understand.

[*There is a long silence during which* MAYOR's *face grows tight and formal and his whole body becomes rigid.*]

MAYOR. [*Crossing to desk.*] I don't wish to speak in this gentleman's presence. [*Sits desk chair.*]

CORELL. [*Rises.*] You have no right to say this. [*Crosses L. to* MAYOR.] I am a soldier like the rest. I just don't wear a uniform.

MAYOR. I don't wish to speak in this gentleman's presence.

LANSER. Will you leave us now, Mr. Corell?

CORELL. I have a right to be here.

LANSER. [*Sharply.*] Do you out-rank me?

CORELL. Oh! No, sir.

LANSER. Please go, Mr. Corell.

[*For a moment* CORELL *looks at the* MAYOR *and his face is angry, then he turns and goes out the door.*]

WINTER. [*Smiles and chuckles.*] That's worth a paragraph for my history!

LANSER. There are some things we must discuss—first—

[MAYOR *rises. Door to R. opens and straw-haired, red-eyed* ANNIE *enters, crossing R.C.*]

ANNIE. There's soldiers on the back porch, Madame. Just standing there.

LANSER. It's just military procedure. They won't come in.

MADAME. [*Coldly.*] Annie, in the future if you have anything to say, let Joseph bring the message.

ANNIE. [*Defiantly.*] I didn't know but they'd try to get in. They smelled the coffee.

MADAME. [*Coldly.*] Annie!

ANNIE. [*Still belligerently.*] Yes, Madame— [*She looks at* LANSER.] —they smelled the coffee. [*She exits R. and closes door.*]

[MADAME *sits desk chair.*]

LANSER. [*Crossing around R. of sofa.*] May I sit down, Your Excellency? We've been a long time without sleep.

MAYOR. Yes. . . . Yes, of course, sit down.

[*He sits L. end sofa,* LANSER *R. end sofa.*]

LANSER. We want to get along as well as we can. You see, sir, this is more a business venture than anything else. We need your coal mine here, and the fishing. We want to get along with just as little friction as possible.

MAYOR. We've had no news. Can you tell me—what about the rest of the country? What has happened?

LANSER. All taken. It was well planned.

MAYOR. [*Insistently.*] Was there no resistance . . . anywhere?

LANSER. [*Looking at him almost compassionately.*] Yes, there was some resistance. I wish there hadn't been. It only caused bloodshed. We'd planned very carefully.

MAYOR. [*Sticking to his point.*] But there *was* resistance?

LANSER. Yes. . . . And it was foolish to resist. Just as

here, it was destroyed instantly. It was sad and foolish to resist.

WINTER. [*Who has caught some of the* MAYOR's *anxious-
ness about the point.*] Yes . . . foolish, but they re-
sisted.

LANSER. Only a few, and they are gone. The people as a
whole are quiet.

WINTER. But the people don't know yet what has happened.

LANSER. [*A little sternly.*] They are discovering now.
They won't be foolish again. [*His voice changes, takes
on a business-like tone.*] I must get to business. I am very
tired. Before I can sleep, I must make my arrangements.
[*He sits forward.*] The coal from this mine must come
out of the ground and be shipped. We have the tech-
nicians with us. The local people will continue to work
the mine. Is that clear? We do not wish to be harsh.

MAYOR. Yes, that's clear enough. But suppose we don't
want to work the mine?

LANSER. [*Tightly.*] I hope you will want to, because
you *must*.

MAYOR. And if we won't?

LANSER. [*Rising.*] You *must!* [*Crossing to R. end sofa.*]
This is an orderly people. They don't want trouble. [*He
waits for the* MAYOR's *reply, and none comes.*] Isn't that
so, sir?

MAYOR. I don't know. They're orderly under our government. I don't know what they'll be under yours. We've
built our government over a long time.

LANSER. [*Quickly.*] We know that. We're going to keep
your government. You will still be the Mayor. You will
give the orders, you will penalize and reward. Then we
won't have trouble.

MAYOR. [*Looking helplessly at* WINTER.] What do you
think?

WINTER. I don't know. I'd expect trouble. This might be a bitter people.

MAYOR. I don't know, either. [*He turns to* LANSER.] Perhaps you know, sir. Or maybe it might be different from anything you know. Some accept leaders and obey them. But my people elected me. They made me and they can unmake me! Perhaps they will do that, when they think I've gone over to you.

LANSER. [*Ominously.*] You will be doing them a service if you keep them in order.

MAYOR. A service?

LANSER. [*Crossing to front of sofa—sits.*] It's your duty to protect them. They'll be in danger if they are rebellious. If they work they will be safe.

MAYOR. But suppose they don't want to be safe?

LANSER. Then you must think for them.

MAYOR. [*A little proudly.*] They don't like to have others think for them. Maybe they are different from your people?

[JOSEPH *enters quickly, crosses D.R., leans forward bursting to speak.*]

MADAME. [*Rises, steps in.*] What is it, Joseph? Get the silver box of cigarettes.

JOSEPH. Pardon, Your Excellency.

MAYOR. What do you want, Joseph?

JOSEPH. [*Excitedly.*] It's Annie, sir.

MADAME. What's the matter with her?

JOSEPH. Annie doesn't like soldiers on the back porch.

LANSER. Are they making trouble?

JOSEPH. They're looking through the door at Annie, sir. She hates that.

LANSER. [*Sighing.*] They are carrying out orders. They're doing no harm.

[MAYOR *looks at* MADAME *helplessly.*]

JOSEPH. Well, Annie hates to be stared at, sir. She's getting angry.

MADAME. Joseph, you tell Annie to mind her temper.

JOSEPH. [*With a gesture of resignation.*] Yes, Madame. [*He turns, shrugs at* WINTER, *then exits R.*]

[MADAME *crosses to desk chair, sits.*]

LANSER. [*His eyes dropping with weariness.*] There is one other thing, Your Excellency. Will it be possible for my staff and me to stay here?

MAYOR. [*Uneasily, a look at* MADAME.] It's a small place. There are larger and more comfortable houses.

LANSER. It isn't that, sir. We have found that when a staff lives under the roof of the local authority, there is more . . . tranquility.

MAYOR. [*A little angrily.*] You mean . . . the people sense there is collaboration.

LANSER. Yes, I suppose that's it. [JOSEPH *comes in with silver box of cigarettes, opens it ostentatiously in front of* LANSER. MADAME *rises to watch. He takes one and* JOSEPH *just as ostentatiously lights it, showing* MADAME *the match he struck on box before lighting cigarette.* LANSER *inhales deeply.* JOSEPH *leaves box on table R. of sofa, exits R.*]

MAYOR. [*Looks hopelessly at* WINTER *and* WINTER *can offer him nothing but a wry smile.* MAYOR *speaks softly.*] Am I permitted . . . to refuse?

LANSER. [*Taking a deep puff on cigarette.*] I'm sorry. No.

MAYOR. The people will not like it.

LANSER. [*As though he speaks to a recalcitrant child.*] Always the people. The people are disarmed. They have no say in this.

MAYOR. [*Shaking his head.*] You do not know, sir!

[*From door R. come the following sounds:*]

FIRST SOLDIER. Look out!
SECOND SOLDIER. It's boiling!

[JOSEPH *enters running.*]

THIRD SOLDIER. Jump!

[*The splash of water, the clang of a pan, and a sharp cry from a soldier.*]

JOSEPH. [*Excitedly.*] Madame! Annie!
MADAME. [*Rises, crosses above sofa, running.*] Annie! [*Exits R.*]
MAYOR. [*Crossing above sofa, to* JOSEPH.] Was anyone hurt?
JOSEPH. The water was boiling! [*Exits R.*]

[*From door R. comes the following:*]

ANNIE. You get out of here! Out of my kitchen! I'll show you!
MADAME. Annie, you behave yourself!
FIRST SOLDIER. Grab her! Get hold of her!
MADAME. Annie!
ANNIE. Let go of me!
MADAME. Annie, you stop that!

[*A sharp thud of someone being thrown to the floor, and a cry from a soldier as though he had been bitten.*]

LANSER. [*Getting up heavily, crosses to desk, speaks angrily.*] Have you no control over your servants, sir?
MAYOR. [*Smiling.*] Very little. Annie is a good cook when she's happy.
LANSER. [*Wearily.*] We just want to do our job. You must discipline your cook.
MAYOR. I can't. She'll quit.
LANSER. This is an emergency. She can't quit.
WINTER. [*Very much amused.*] Then she'll throw water.

[*The door, R., opens and a* SOLDIER *enters, crosses D.R.*]

SOLDIER. Shall I arrest this woman, sir?

LANSER. Was anyone hurt?

SOLDIER. Yes, sir, scalded, and one man bitten. We are holding her down, sir.

LANSER. [*Helplessly, leans against desk.*] Oh! Release her and go outside.

SOLDIER. Very good, sir. [*Crosses R. to door.*]

LANSER. Off the porch.

[SOLDIER *exits and closes door behind him.*]

LANSER. I could lock her up. I could have her shot.

MAYOR. Then we'd have no cook.

LANSER. [*Putting out cigarette in desk ash-tray.*] Our instructions are to get along with your people. I'm very tired, sir. I must have some sleep. Please cooperate with us for the good of all.

MAYOR. [*Thoughtfully.*] I don't know. The people are confused and so am I!

LANSER. But will you try to cooperate?

MAYOR. [*Slowly, crossing to front sofa.*] I don't know. When the town makes up its mind what it wants to do I will probably do that. [*Sits sofa.*]

LANSER. You're the authority.

MAYOR. Authority is in the town. That means we cannot act as quickly as you can . . . but when the direction is set . . . we act all together. I don't know . . . yet!

LANSER. I hope we can get along together. I hope we can depend on you to help. Look at it realistically. There's nothing you can do to stop us. And I don't like to think of the means the military must take to keep order. [*Crosses U.C. to table for helmet.*]

[MAYOR *is silent, looking at floor.*]

MADAME. [*Enter from R. with cup of coffee, crosses to R. of* MAYOR.] She's all right. [*Hands him cup.*]

[LANSER *crosses D.L., puts on helmet.*]

MAYOR. [*Taking cup.*] Thank you, my dear.
LANSER. I hope we can depend on you.
MAYOR. I don't know—yet.

[LANSER *bows, turns sharply, exits U.L., followed by* CORPORAL. MADAME *sits R. of* MAYOR *on sofa, straightens his hair.*]

CURTAIN

PART ONE

SCENE II

SCENE: *The same room a few days later. Piled military equipment and canvas-wrapped bundles are lying around. The sofa and end-tables as well as the chess-table, pedestal and vase of ferns have been removed. The 3 gold-framed pictures that hung above the* MAYOR'S *desk have been taken down. The drapes and curtains which hung at the windows have been removed. On the mantel stands only a clock and an ash-tray. The* MAYOR'S *desk has maps, a microscope, several specimens of rock and ore. At the windows are three odd chairs. Three more chairs are placed at the table in C. of room. This is the same table that was at the windows in the preceding scene.*

Since most of the staff enter this scene, they might be described thus:

MAJOR HUNTER, *the second in command, is a short wide-shouldered mining engineer . . . a man of figures and a formula. If there had been no war, no one would have thought of making a soldier of him. None of the humor, or the music, or the mysticism of higher mathematics ever entered his head. His drawing-board and his geologic hammer were his most important possessions. He had been married twice, and he did not know why each of his wives became very nervous before she left him.* HUNTER'S *brows are heavy and his eyes small and bright and wide-set.*

CAPTAIN BENTICK, *who comes into the scene only as a corpse, was a family man. A lover of dogs and pink children and Christmas. He was too old to be a Captain,*

21

but a curious lack of ambition has kept him in that rank. When there is no war, he admires British country gentlemen very much, wears English clothes, keeps English dogs, smokes a special pipe mixture sent him from London, in an English pipe. He subscribes to those country magazines which extol flower gardening, and continually argues about the merit of English and Gordon Setters. Once he wrote a letter to the Times *concerning grass drying in the Midlands. He signed it, "Edmund Twitchel, Esquire" and the* Times *had printed it.*

CAPTAIN LOFT *is truly a military man. As much a Captain as one can imagine. He lives and breathes his Captaincy. He has no unmilitary moments. He can click his heels as perfectly as a dancer does. He knows every kind of military courtesy, and insists on using it all. Generals are afraid of him because he knows more about the deportment of soldiers than they do. He believes that a soldier is the highest development of animal life, and if he considers God at all, he thinks of him as an old and honored General, retired and gray, living among remembered battles.*

LIEUTENANT PRACKLE *is an undergraduate . . . a snotnose; a lieutenant trained in the politics of the day, he believes the great new system invented by a genius so great that he has never bothered to verify its results.* LIEUTENANT PRACKLE *is a devil with women. If he lived in America he might well be giving his all every Saturday to his Alma Mater, for war to him is rather like a football game, and so far he has enjoyed it immensely. He is a sentimental young man, and he considers himself a cynical one. He carries a lock of hair in his watch, which is constantly getting loose and clogging the balance wheel.* PRACKLE *is a pleasant dancing partner, but nevertheless he can scold like the leader, can brood like the leader; he hates degenerate art, and has destroyed* several canvasses with his own hands. PRACKLE *has several blonde sisters, of whom he is proud and about whom he is sensitive. He has caused a commotion on occasion when he thought they were insulted. His sisters are a little upset about it, because they are afraid someone might set out to prove the insults, which would not be hard to do.* LIEUTENANT PRACKLE *once spent two weeks' furlough attempting to seduce* LIEUTENANT TONDER'S *blonde sister, a buxom girl who loved to be seduced by older men who did not muss her hair as* LIEUTENANT PRACKLE *did.*

LIEUTENANT TONDER *is a different kind of sophomore. A dark and bitter and cynical poet, who dreams of the perfect ideal love of elevated young men for poor girls. Once he wooed and won a beautiful and smelly waif, and that was before the application of Sulphanilamide. He broods often on death, his own particularly, lighted by a fair setting sun which glints on broken military equipment, his men standing silently around him, with low-sunk heads, while over a fat cloud gallop the Valkyrie to the thunderous strains of Wagnerian music. And he has his dying words ready to speak.*

There are the men of the staff, each one playing war as children play run-sheep-run, and their wars so far have been play . . . fine weapons and fine planning against unarmed, planless and surprised enemies. Under pressure they were capable of courage or cowardice, as anyone is.

COLONEL LANSER, *among them all, knows what war really is. He had been in Belgium and France twenty years before, and he tries not to think what he knows; that war is hatred and treachery, the muddling of incompetent generals, torture and killing and sick tiredness, until at last it is over and nothing has changed except for new weariness and new hatreds.* LANSER *is a soldier; given orders*

*to carry out, he will carry them out. And he will try to
put aside his own sick memories of war.
As the curtain rises it is morning. R. of the large
center table* MAJOR HUNTER *sits. He is balancing his
drawing-board against the edge of the table and against
his lap. He works with a T-Square triangle and drawing
pencil. The drawing-board is unsteady and unsatis-
factory to work on. Attempting to draw a line, his pencil slips.*

HUNTER. [*Calling sharply.*] Prackle, Lieutenant Prackle!

[*The bedroom door opens,* PRACKLE *comes out. His tunic
is off, and half his face is covered with shaving cream.
He holds the shaving brush in his hand.*]

PRACKLE. Yes, Major.

HUNTER. [*Jiggling his drawing-board.*] Hasn't the tripod for my board turned up in the baggage yet?

PRACKLE. [*Crossing in.*] I don't know. I didn't look.

HUNTER. Well, look now, will you? It's bad enough to
have to work in this light. I'll have to draw this again
before I ink it.

PRACKLE. [*Crossing to door L.*] I'll find it as soon as I
finish shaving.

HUNTER. [*Irritably.*] It seems to me this railroad siding
is more important than your looks. See if there is a tripod
case in there.

[PRACKLE *exits L. The door to stairway opens and* CAP-
TAIN LOFT *enters.*]

LOFT. [*Wears helmet, a pair of field-glasses, side-arm,
and various little leather cases strung all over him. He
begins to remove his equipment as soon as he enters.*]

You know Bentick is crazy. He was going on duty in a fatigue cap, right down the street. [*He puts his glasses on table, takes off his helmet and gas-mask bag. A little pile of equipment begins to heap up on the table.*]

HUNTER. Don't leave that stuff there. I have to work here. [LOFT *places his things on chair above table.*] Why shouldn't he wear a fatigue cap? There hasn't been any trouble. I get sick of these damn tin hats. You can't see out from under them.

LOFT. [*Grimly. Draws himself up when he speaks, as though he were making a report.*] It's bad business to leave the helmet off. Bad for the people here. We must maintain a military standard of alertness, and never vary it.

HUNTER. What makes you think so?

LOFT. [*Draws himself a little higher, thins his mouth with certainty. Sooner or later everyone wants to punch* LOFT *in the nose for his sureness about things.*] I don't think it. I was paraphrasing Manual X12 on Deportment in Occupied Countries. It is very carefully worked out. The leaders have considered everything. [*He starts to say "you," and then changes it to—*] Every soldier should read X12 very carefully. [*Sits chair L. of table.*]

HUNTER. I wonder whether the man who wrote it was ever in an occupied country. These people seem harmless enough.

[PRACKLE *comes through door and crosses to R. window, his face still half-covered with dry shaving soap. He carries a brown canvas tube and an iron tripod base.*]

PRACKLE. Here it is, Major.

HUNTER. Unpack it, will you, and set it up.

[PRACKLE *opens bag, takes out a metal rod and puts it in the base.* HUNTER *takes his drawing equipment to chair at window.* LIEUTENANT TONDER *enters from R. with cup of coffee, crosses to chair vacated by* HUNTER, *sits and looks at the plan on board.*]

LOFT. You have soap on your face, Lieutenant.

PRACKLE. Yes, sir. I was shaving when the Major asked me to get the tripod.

LOFT. Better get it off; the Colonel might see you.

PRACKLE. Oh, he wouldn't mind; he doesn't care about that.

LOFT. Better wipe it off.

[PRACKLE *exits L.* TONDER *is looking at* HUNTER's *board and points to a drawing in the corner of the board.* HUNTER *sets a chair at tripod.*]

TONDER. That's a nice-looking bridge, Major, but where are we going to build a bridge?

HUNTER. [*Crosses to table for board, looks down at drawing and then at* TONDER.] Huh? Oh, that isn't any bridge we're going to build. Up here is the work drawing. [*Takes board to tripod.*]

TONDER. [*Rises, crosses U. to window.*] Well, what are you doing with the bridge, then?

HUNTER. [*A little embarrassedly, as he readies his board for work, sitting behind it.*] I was just playing with that. You know in my backyard at home I've got a model railroad line. I was going to bridge a little creek for it. Brought the line right down to the creek, but I never did get the bridge built. I thought I would kind of work it out while I was away.

[PRACKLE *enters buttoning his tunic. He has a folded rotogravure page from his pocket. It is a picture of an actress, or any one of a number of girls who are all legs, and dress and eyelashes. A well-developed blonde in black open-work stockings, and a low bodice. She peeps over a black lace fan.* TONDER *crosses L.C.*]

PRACKLE. [*Holding her up.*] Isn't she something?

[LOFT *glances at picture then turns back to his work at table.* HUNTER *goes on drawing.*]

TONDER. [*Looks critically at picture.*] I don't like her.

PRACKLE. What don't you like about her?

TONDER. I just don't like her. [*Crossing R. below table to arm-chair at fireplace.*] What do you want her picture for?

PRACKLE. Because I do like her. I bet you do, too.

TONDER. No, I don't.

PRACKLE. You mean to say you wouldn't go out with her if you could?

TONDER. No. [*Sits arm-chair.*]

PRACKLE. You're just crazy. [*Goes to wall above desk L.*] I'm just going to stick her up here and let you brood about her for a while. [*He nails picture on wall with a rock from desk.*]

LOFT. [*Busy with his work.*] I don't think that looks very well out here, Lieutenant. It would make a bad impression on the local people. Better take it down.

HUNTER. [*Looks up from his board for the first time.*] Take what down? [*He follows their eyes to picture.*] Who's that?

PRACKLE. She's an actress. [*Sits desk chair admiring picture.*]

HUNTER. Oh, you know her?

TONDER. She's a tramp.

HUNTER. Oh, then you know her?

PRACKLE. [*He seems only now to have understood* TONDER. *Rises, steps in.*] Say, how do you know she's a tramp?

TONDER. She looks like a tramp. [*Rises, places cup on mantel.*]

PRACKLE. Do you know her?

TONDER. No, and I don't want to. [*Crosses to R. of* HUNTER, *watching him work*]

PRACKLE. [*Begins to say.*] Then, how do you know . . . ?

LOFT. [*Breaking in, looking at him.*] Take the picture down. Put it up over your bed if you want to. This is official here. [PRACKLE *looks at him mutinously.*] That's an order.

[PRACKLE *takes down picture, sits desk chair, looking at it.*]

TONDER. [*Looking over* HUNTER's *shoulder again.*] What's that?

HUNTER. [*Coming slowly out of his work.*] That's a new line I'm building from the mine to the ships. Got to get the coal moving. It's a big job. I'm glad the people here are calm and sensible.

LOFT. They are calm and sensible because *we* are calm and sensible. I think we can take credit for that. That is why I keep harping on procedure. It is very carefully worked out.

PRACKLE. [*Tries cheerily to change the subject to save his face.*] There are some pretty girls in this town, too. As soon as we get settled down, I'm going to get acquainted with a few.

LOFT. You'd better read X12. There is a chapter dealing with sexual matters.

[PRACKLE *folds picture and puts it in his pocket. Door U.L. opens and* LANSER *enters, removing his coat as he comes in. His staff gives him military courtesy, but it is not rigid.*]

LANSER. Captain Loft, will you go down and relieve Bentick at the mine. He isn't feeling well. Says he is dizzy.

[PRACKLE *takes his coat and helmet into bedroom L.* TONDER *crosses to chair at window, sits looking out.*]

LOFT. [*Getting into his coat and equipment.*] Yes, sir. May I suggest, sir, that I only recently came off duty?

LANSER. [*Inspecting him closely.*] I hope you don't mind going?

LOFT. Not at all, sir. I just mentioned it for the record.

LANSER. [*Relaxing and chuckling. Sits against desk.*] You like to be mentioned in the record.

LOFT. It does no harm, sir.

LANSER. [*Lighting cigarette.*] And when you have enough mentions there will be a little dangler on your chest.

LOFT. They are the milestones in a military career, sir.

LANSER. Yes, I guess they are. But . . . they won't be the ones you'll remember.

LOFT. Sir?

LANSER. You'll know what I mean later . . . perhaps.

LOFT. [*Putting on his equipment rapidly.*] Yes sir. [*He goes out doors U.L.*]

LANSER. [*Watches him go with a little amusement. Quietly.*] There is a born soldier.

HUNTER. [*Poises his pencil and looks up from board.*] A born ass.

LANSER. [*Crossing to table—looks at reports.*] No. He is being a soldier the way another man would be a politician. [PRACKLE *enters from L.*] He'll be on the General Staff before long. He'll look down on the war from above and so he'll always love it.

PRACKLE. When do you think the war will be over, sir?

LANSER. Over?

[TONDER *turns to them.*]

PRACKLE. [*Stepping in.*] How soon will we win?

LANSER. [*Shaking his head.*] Oh, I don't know. The enemy is still in the world.

PRACKLE. But we'll lick them.

LANSER. [*Crossing to fireplace.*] Yes?

PRACKLE. Won't we?

LANSER. [*Smiling a little sadly.*] Yes . . . Yes . . . [*Turns to him.*] We always do.

PRACKLE. [*Excitedly. Crosses to table, sits chair L. of table.*] Well, if it is quiet around Christmas, do you think there might be some furloughs?

[TONDER *rises, crosses D. to table.*]

LANSER. I don't know. The orders will have to come from home. Do you want to get home for Christmas?

PRACKLE. Well, I'd like to.

LANSER. Maybe you will . . . Maybe you will.

TONDER. We won't drop out of this occupation, will we, sir . . . after the war is over?

LANSER. I don't know. Why?

TONDER. [*Sits chair above table.*] Well, it's a nice country. Nice people. Our men, some of them, might even settle here.

LANSER. [*Jokingly.*] You've seen a place you like?

TONDER. [*A little embarrassed.*] Well, there are some beautiful little farms here. If four or five of them were thrown together, it would make a nice place to settle.

LANSER. You have no family land at home, then?

TONDER. Not any more, sir. The inflation took it away.

LANSER. [*Tiring now of talking to children.*] Ah, well. We still have a war to fight. We still have coal to ship. [*Crossing to* HUNTER.] Suppose we wait until it is over, before we build up estates. Hunter, your steel will be in tomorrow. You can get your tracks started this week.

[*A knock at door U.L.* CORPORAL *enters.*]

CORPORAL. Mr. Corell wishes to see you, sir.

LANSER. Send him in. [CORPORAL *exits.* LANSER, *speaking to the others, crossing to R. end of table.*] He worked hard here for us. We might have some trouble with him.

TONDER. Didn't he do a good job?

LANSER. Yes, he did. But he won't be popular with the people here. [*Sits chair R. of table.*] I wonder if he will be popular with us.

TONDER. He deserves credit.

LANSER. Yes, I suppose he does. But that won't make him popular.

CORELL. [*Comes in rubbing his hands. He radiates good will and good fellowship. He is dressed in a black business suit. On his head there is a patch of white bandage, stuck into his hair with a cross of adhesive tape. He crosses D. to L. of* PRACKLE.] Good morning, Colonel. I should have called yesterday, after the little misunderstanding. But I know how busy you are.

LANSER. Good morning. [*With a circular gesture of his hand.*] This is my staff, Mr. Corell.

CORELL. Fine boys. [*Slaps* PRACKLE *on the back, who rises and exits L.* CORELL *crosses D.L.*] They did a good job. I did my best to prepare for them.

[HUNTER *takes out an inking pen, dips it, and begins to ink in his drawing.*]

LANSER. [*Rises, crosses R. to fireplace.* CORELL *crosses to chair L. of table.*] You did very well. I wish we hadn't killed those six men, though.

CORELL. Well, six men isn't much for a town like this, with a coal mine, too.

LANSER. [*Sternly.*] I don't mind killing people if that finishes it. [*Turns to him.*] But sometimes it doesn't finish it.

CORELL. [*Looking sideways at* TONDER *and* HUNTER.] Perhaps if we could talk alone, Colonel—?

LANSER. Yes, if you wish. Lieutenant Tonder, will you go to your room, please. [TONDER *rises, bows, exits L.* CORELL *then gestures toward* HUNTER.] Major Hunter is working. He doesn't hear anything when he's working. [HUNTER *looks up from his board, smiles quietly and looks down again.* LANSER, *not quite at his ease, crossing in to R.C.*] Well, here we are. Won't you sit down?

CORELL. Thank you, Sir. [CORELL *takes off coat and hat, places them on chair above table, sits down chair L. of table.*]

LANSER. [*Studies bandage on* CORELL'S *head. Speaks bluntly.*] Have they tried to kill you already?

CORELL. [*Fingers the bandage.*] This? Oh, no. This was a stone that fell from the cliff in the hills this morning.

LANSER. You are sure it wasn't thrown?

CORELL. What do you mean? These aren't fierce people. They haven't had a war for a hundred years. They've forgotten about fighting.

LANSER. [*Crossing L. to desk.*] Well, you've lived among them, you ought to know. But if you are safe, these people are different from any in the world. I've helped to occupy countries before. I was in Belgium twenty years ago, and in France. [*Sits against desk, shakes head a little as though to clear it. To* CORELL, *gruffly.*] You did a good job. I have mentioned your work in my report.

CORELL. [*Turns to him.*] Thank you, sir. I did my best.

LANSER. [*A little wearily, places foot on desk chair.*] Well, now what shall we do with you? Would you like to go back to the Capitol? You can go in a coal barge if you are in a hurry, or in a destroyer if you want to wait.

CORELL. I don't want to go back. My place is here.

LANSER. I haven't very many men. I can't give you a bodyguard.

CORELL. But I don't need a bodyguard. I tell you these are not violent people.

[LANSER *looks at bandage and says nothing.*]

HUNTER. [*Glancing up from board.*] I suggest you start wearing a helmet. [*He looks down at his work again.*]

CORELL. [*Looks at* HUNTER, *then rises, steps to* LANSER.] I wanted particularly to talk to you, Colonel. I thought I might help with the Civil administration.

LANSER. [*Walks to the R. end of table—looks at* HUNTER.] What have you in mind?

CORELL. Well, you must have a Mayor you can trust. I thought perhaps Orden might step down now, and . . . Well, if I were to take over his office . . . we could work very nicely together.

LANSER. [*His eyes seem to grow large and bright. He turns to* CORELL *and speaks sharply.*] Have you mentioned this in your report to the Capitol?

CORELL. Well, yes . . . naturally, in my analysis . . .

LANSER. [*Interrupting.*] Have you talked to any of the town people since we arrived—outside the Mayor, that is?

CORELL. [*Giving ground.*] Well, no. You see, they are still a bit startled. They didn't expect it. [LANSER *crosses to above table, looking at* HUNTER. *Chuckling.*] No, sir, they didn't expect it. [*Sits chair L. of table.*]

LANSER. [*Pressing his point.*] So you don't really know what is going on in their heads?

CORELL. Why, they've had a shock. They're going to be all right.

LANSER. You don't know what they think of you?

CORELL. I have lots of friends here. I know everyone.

LANSER. [*Takes a step to him.*] Has anyone bought anything in your store this morning?

CORELL. Naturally, business is at a standstill.

LANSER. [*Suddenly relaxes. He speaks quietly.*] Yours is a difficult and brave branch of the service. [*Crosses U. to* HUNTER.] It should be greatly rewarded.

CORELL. Thank you, sir.

LANSER. You'll have their hatred in time.

CORELL. I can stand that, sir. They are the enemy.

LANSER. [*Hesitating a long moment before he speaks. Says almost in a whisper, turning to* CORELL.] You will not even have *our* respect.

CORELL. [*Jumping to his feet.*] The Leader has said all branches are equally honorable.

LANSER. [*Still very quietly.*] I hope the Leader is right. I hope he can read the minds of soldiers. [*Crosses to chair R. end table, sits. Pulls himself together.*] Now. We must come to exactness. I am in charge here. I must maintain order and discipline. To do that I must know what is in the minds of these people. I must anticipate revolt.

CORELL. [*Sits in chair L. of table.*] I can find out what you wish to know, sir. As Mayor here, I will be very effective.

LANSER. Orden is more than Mayor. He *is* the people. He will think what they think. By watching him I will know them. He must stay. That is my judgment.

CORELL. My place is here, sir. I have made my place.

LANSER. I have no orders about this. I must use my own judgment. I think you will never again know what is going on here. I think no one will speak to you. No one will be near to you, except those people who live on money. I think without a bodyguard you will be in great danger. I prefer that you go back to the Capitol.

CORELL. My work, sir, merits better treatment than being sent away.

LANSER. [*Slowly.*] Yes, it does. But to the larger work I think you are only in the way. If you are not hated yet, you will be. In any little revolt you will be the first to be killed. I suggest that you go back.

CORELL. [*Rises, stiffly.*] You will, of course, permit me to wait for a reply from the Capitol?

LANSER. Of course. [*Rises.*] But I shall recommend that you go back for your own safety. Frankly . . . you have no further value here. [*Crossing.*] But . . . well, there must be other plans in other countries. Perhaps you will go now to some new town, win new confidence . . . a greater responsibility. I will recommend you highly for your work here.

CORELL. [*His eyes shining with the praise.*] Thank you, sir. I have worked hard. Perhaps you are right. [*Crosses to chair above table, puts on coat.*] But I will wait for the reply from the Capitol.

LANSER. [*His voice tight and his eyes slitted. Harshly, crossing to table.*] Wear a helmet. Keep indoors. Do not go out at night, and above all do not drink. Trust no woman or any man. You understand?

CORELL. [*Smiling as though* LANSER *were a petulant child. Crossing D. to below table.*] I don't think you understand. I have a little house, a country girl waits on me. I even think she is fond of me. These are peaceful people.

LANSER. There are no peaceful people. When will you learn it? There are no friendly people. Can't you understand that? We have invaded this country. You, by what they call treachery, prepared for us. [*His face grows red and his voice rises.*] Can't you understand that we are at war with these people? [*Crosses U.R.*]

CORELL. [*A little smugly.*] We have defeated them.

LANSER. [*He goes on as though he were instructing a class. Crosses to him above table.*] A defeat is a momentary thing. A defeat doesn't last. We were defeated and now we are back. Defeat means nothing. Can't you understand that? Do you know what they are whispering behind doors?

CORELL. Do you?

[*The door R. closes suddenly. Both men turn to look.*]

LANSER. No. [*Crosses to fireplace.*]

CORELL. [*Crosses quickly to door R., opens it, looks out, then closes it and crosses D.R. to* LANSER. *Insinuatingly.*] Are you afraid, Colonel? [LANSER *turns to him.*] Should our Commander be afraid?

LANSER. [*Sitting down heavily in arm-chair.*] Maybe that's it. [*He says disgustedly.*] I am tired of people who have not been at war who know all about it. [*He is silent for a moment.*] I remember a little old woman in Brussels. Sweet face, white hair . . . Delicate old hands. [*He seems to see the figure in front of him.*] She used to sing our songs to us in a quivering voice. She always knew where to find a cigarette or a virgin. [LANSER *catches himself as though he had been asleep.*] We didn't know her son had been executed. When we finally shot her, she had killed twelve men with a long black hat-pin.

CORELL. [*Eagerly.*] But you shot her.

LANSER. Of course we shot her!

CORELL. And the murders stopped?

LANSER. No . . . the murders didn't stop. And when finally we retreated, the people cut off stragglers. They burned some. And they gouged the eyes from some. And some they even crucified.

CORELL. These are not good things to say.

LANSER. They are not good things to remember.

CORELL. You should not be in command if you are afraid. [*Crosses away from* LANSER *to* L. *end of table.*]

LANSER. [*Softly.*] I know how to fight.

CORELL. [*Turns to him.*] You don't talk this way to the young officers?

LANSER. [*Shaking his head.*] No. They wouldn't believe me.

CORELL. [*In anger and fear. Crossing toward him.*] Why do you tell me, then?

LANSER. Because your work is done. Your work is done.

[*The door* U.L. *bursts open.* CAPTAIN LOFT *enters. He is rigid and cold and military.*]

LOFT. There is trouble, sir.

LANSER. [*Rises.*] Trouble?

LOFT. Captain Bentick has been hurt.

LANSER. Oh . . . yes. [*Crosses to* C. STRETCHER BEARERS *enter, carrying a figure covered with blankets.* LOFT *crosses to below desk.* CORELL *crosses above table.*] How badly is he hurt?

LOFT. [*Stiffly.*] I don't know.

[PRACKLE *enters from bedroom and stands in doorway.*]

LANSER. Put him in there. [*He points to bedroom* L. *The* BEARERS *exit* L. *with their burden.* PRACKLE *exits ahead of them.* LANSER *follows them off,* HUNTER *crosses to front table.* CORELL *crosses* D.L. *After a pause* LANSER *enters, stands at door.*] Who killed him?

LOFT. A miner.

[HUNTER *crosses back to his drawing-board.*]

LANSER. Why?

LOFT. I was there, sir.

LANSER. Well, make your report, then. Make your report, dammit!

LOFT. [*Draws himself up and says formally.*] I had just relieved Captain Bentick as the Colonel ordered. Captain Bentick was about to leave to come here, when I had some trouble with a miner. He wanted to quit. When I ordered him to work, he rushes at me with his pick. Captain Bentick tried to interfere.

[CORELL *crosses to chair for hat, then exits U.L.* LOFT *turns to watch* CORELL.]

LANSER. [*Crosses to C. Sternly.*] You captured the man?

LOFT. Yes, sir.

LANSER. [*Slowly crossing to fireplace, speaks as though to himself.*] So it starts again. We'll shoot this man and make twenty new enemies. It's the only thing we know. The only thing we know.

LOFT. [*Crossing in to C.*] What did you say, sir?

LANSER. Nothing. Nothing at all, I was just thinking. [*He turns to* LOFT.] Please give my compliments to Mayor Orden and my request that he see me at once.

[LOFT *turns, exits U.L.* HUNTER, *looking up, dries his inking pen carefully and puts it away in its velvet-lined box.*]

CURTAIN

PART ONE

SCENE III

SCENE: *The same. Two days later. The disintegration of the room is under way. There is some military equipment about, but a desolateness is apparent from the arrangement of the furniture. The console table U.R. and the large painting above it have gone. The mantel is bare of dressing. The table used in Scene II has been removed. There are newspapers on the floor around the fireplace. Even the grandfather clock has been moved out. Only the* MAYOR's *desk, chair and the arm-chair R. remain as we first saw them. Five chairs are pushed back against wall U.C., leaving the center of the room quite bare. Three small chairs are D.L. The light is rather cold.*

AT RISE: *Curtain rises on an empty stage, but immediately the door R. is opened by* JOSEPH, *who at once turns his back and begins the manoeuvering of a large dining-room table through the door. He talks to* ANNIE *off-stage, who is helping with the other end of the table. The table is so large that it has been turned on its side to get it through the door at all.*

JOSEPH. [*Edging the legs through door.*] Don't push now, Annie. [*Clears the legs.*] Now push, Annie. Now—

ANNIE. [*Appears in door at other end of table.*] I am.

JOSEPH. Don't scuff the bottom. Lift—lift on it. Steady!

ANNIE. [*A little angrily.*] I am steady.

[*They manoeuver the table through the door and stand it on its legs. It is quite heavy.*]
39

JOSEPH. Now—right over here. Right in the center. [*They put table in C. of room.*] There!

ANNIE. [*Truculently, as they open table for the leaves.*] If His Excellency hadn't told me to do it I wouldn't. What's a dining table want in here!

JOSEPH. [*Gets leaves from U.C., takes them to table.*] The Colonel wants it here. They're going to hold some kind of a trial.

ANNIE. Why don't they hold it down at the City Hall where it belongs?

JOSEPH. I don't know. They do crazy things. It's some kind of way they have. [*They close table.*] Look at this room. There's no way to fix it up with their stuff all over. [*Places 2 chairs from U.C. above table.*]

ANNIE. [*As though she really doesn't want to know; crossing D.L. for a chair.*] What do they want to have a trial for?

JOSEPH. Well—there's talk. People say there was trouble at the mine. Some kind of a fight.

ANNIE. [*Her interest is aroused as she crosses to front table with chair.*] You mean they're going to try one of *us?*

JOSEPH. That's what they say. [*Places chair from U.C. at R. end table.*]

ANNIE. Who?

JOSEPH. [*Places chair from U.C. above table.*] Well, they say Alex Morden got in some kind of trouble at the mine.

ANNIE. [*Crossing D.L. for 2 chairs.*] That's Molly's husband. He never gets in any trouble. He's a good man. What kind of trouble could Alex get into?

JOSEPH. Well, some people say he hit a soldier. [*Places chair from U.C. at L. end table.*]

ANNIE. [*Crossing to front table with 2 chairs.*] It's a time of trouble. Molly Kenderly wouldn't have married a man who hit people. Alex is a good man. The soldiers must have done something to Alex. [*Crosses to fireplace.*]

JOSEPH. [*Crossing C.*] I don't know. Nobody seems to know what happened. I heard— [*Tiptoes to door L., opens it slowly, then closes it, crosses R. to* ANNIE.] — that William Deal and his wife got away last night in a little boat and I heard that somebody hit that man Corell with a rock. Everybody's uneasy.

ANNIE. [*Picking up papers at fireplace and sweeping up.*] Uneasy. You should see my sister. Her boy Robbie got away when they killed the other soldiers. Christine thinks she knows where he'd go back in the hills, but she can't find out if he was hurt or anything. She's going crazy worrying. She even wanted me to ask His Excellency to try to find out. He might be hurt. I can't ask His Excellency.

JOSEPH. I know. [MAYOR *enters U.L., standing in doorway, hears himself mentioned and stops.*] People in the town are worried about His Excellency. They don't know where he stands—soldiers in his house and he hasn't said anything. [MAYOR *crosses in to L. end table.*] And you know—everybody liked Corell and then he was for the soldiers. [WINTER *enters U.L. and stands in doorway.*] People are worried about His Excellency.

MAYOR. [*Looking at table.*] This is right. I guess this is what they want. [*Crosses to desk.* JOSEPH *and* ANNIE *are caught talking about him. They are embarrassed.*] You can tell anyone you see that I haven't gone over to the enemy. I am still the Mayor.

[WINTER *crosses U.C. to windows.*]

JOSEPH. [*Crossing C.*] We didn't mean—
ANNIE. [*Crossing L. to* MAYOR.] Your Excellency—

Christine's boy got away. She thinks he's in the hills and maybe hurt.

MAYOR. Does she know where he is?

ANNIE. She thinks so. About fifteen miles away in the hills.

MAYOR. [*Turns to* JOSEPH.] Would you go?

JOSEPH. Yes, sir.

MAYOR. Then go tonight. And don't let anyone see you go.

JOSEPH. Yes, Your Excellency.

ANNIE. Thank you, Your Excellency. I'll tell Christine.

[JOSEPH *and* ANNIE *exit R. excitedly, and apparently they are going to spread the news.* WINTER *comes silently down and seats himself in one of the chairs above big table.* MAYOR *speaks out of thought.*]

MAYOR. I wonder how much longer I can stay in this position? Which is better——to be thrown out of control or to remain and have the people suspect me?

WINTER. Maybe you could keep control and be with the people, too.

MAYOR. I don't know. The people don't quite trust me and neither does the enemy.

WINTER. You trust yourself, don't you? There is no doubt in your mind where you stand?

MAYOR. Doubt? No, I'm the Mayor. [*Rises, crosses to L. end table.*] I don't understand many things. [*He points to table.*] I don't know why they have to bring this trial in here. They are going to try Alex Morden here for murder. You know Alex. He has that pretty wife, Molly.

WINTER. I remember. She taught in a grammar school before she was married. Yes, I remember her. She was so pretty she hated to get glasses when she needed them. Well, I guess Alex killed an officer all right. Nobody has questioned that.

MAYOR. [*Bitterly, as he sits chair L. of table.*] Of course, no one questions it. But why do they try him? Why don't they shoot him? We don't try them for killing our soldiers. A trial implies right or wrong, doubt or certainty. There is none of that here. Why must they try him— and in my house?

WINTER. I would guess it is for the show. There is an idea about that if you go through the form of a thing you have it. They'll have a trial and hope to convince the people that there is justice involved. Alex did kill the Captain.

MAYOR. Yes, I know.

WINTER. And if it comes from your house, where the people have always expected justice . . .

[*He is interrupted by the door opening R. A young* WOMAN *enters. She is about thirty, and quite pretty. She is dressed simply, neatly. She is excited. This is* MOLLY MORDEN.]

MOLLY. [*Quickly, crossing in to R. end table.*] Annie told me just to come right in, sir.

MAYOR. [*Rises, looks at her.*] Why, of course.

MOLLY. They say Alex will be tried and . . . shot. They say you will try him.

MAYOR. [*Looks up quickly at* WINTER.] Who says this?

MOLLY. [*Crossing C.*] The people in the town. [*She holds herself very straight. Her voice is half-pleading and half-demanding.*] You wouldn't do that, would you, sir?

MAYOR. [*Crossing L. to desk chair.*] How could the people know what I don't know about myself?

WINTER. [*Quietly.*] That's a mystery . . . how the people know. How the truth of things gets out.

MOLLY. [*Coming near to him.*] Alex is not a murdering man. He is a quick-tempered man. He has never broken the law. He is a respected man.

[WINTER *crosses to R. end of table.*]

MAYOR. [*Crossing to her.*] I know. [*He is silent for a moment.*] I've known Alex since he was a little boy. I knew his father and his grandfather. His grandfather was a bear hunter in the old days. Did you know that?

MOLLY. [*Ignores his words.*] You won't sentence Alex?

MAYOR. No. How could I sentence him?

MOLLY. [*Turns away from him.*] The people said you would for the sake of order.

MAYOR. [*A step to her.*] Do the people want order, Molly?

MOLLY. [*Turns to him.*] They want to be free.

MAYOR. Do they know how to go about it? Do they know what methods to use against this armed enemy?

MOLLY. [*Her chin comes up.*] No, sir. But I think the people want to show these soldiers that they aren't beaten.

WINTER. [*Crossing to fireplace.*] They've had no chance to fight. [MOLLY *looks at* WINTER.] It's no fight to go against machine guns.

MAYOR. [*Crosses to her, takes her hand. She turns to him.*] When you know what the people want to do, will you tell me, Molly?

MOLLY. [*Looks at him suspiciously, takes away her hand, turns and moves away from him.*] Yes. [*Unconvincingly.*]

MAYOR. You mean no. You don't trust me.

MOLLY. [*Defiantly, turns to him.*] How about Alex?

MAYOR. I will not sentence him. He has committed no crime against our people.

MOLLY. [*Fearfully.*] Will they . . . kill Alex? [*Looks at* WINTER. *He crosses to arm-chair, sits. She turns to* MAYOR.]

MAYOR. [*Stares blankly at her for a moment.*] Dear
child, my poor child!

MOLLY. [*She stands rigidly, her face very tight.*] Thank
you. [MAYOR *comes near her.*] Don't touch me. Please
don't touch me. [*Crosses U.L. As she reaches door, she
runs out.*] Please don't touch me! [MAYOR *turns as
though to follow her.*]

WINTER. Let her go.

[MAYOR *stops.* MADAME *comes in door R.*]

MADAME. [*Crossing C. front table.*] I don't know how I
can run the house. It's more people than the house can
stand. Annie's angry all the time.

MAYOR. [*Turns to her.*] Sara—listen to me.

MADAME. [*In amazement.*] I don't know what I'm going
to do with Annie.

MAYOR. Hush! Sara, I want you to go to Alex Morden's
house. You know where it is. Do you understand? I want
you to stay with Molly . . . while she needs you. Don't
talk; just stay with her.

MADAME. I have a hundred things—

MAYOR. [*A little angry.*] I can't understand you. They
are going to kill Alex. [*Crosses to chair R. front table,
sits.*] I can't see how you can rattle on—the house—the
servants—

MADAME. [*Turns and looks at him with affection. For a
moment a mask seems to drop. When she speaks it is
in a kind of self-revelation that only comes in great emotion.*] Dear—I am doing what I can. There must be
some to do the regular daily thing. When there is a
funeral some people mourn and then there are some
women in the kitchen cooking. Do you think they feel
death less or do you think they know that life goes on
in death, that life balances death?

MAYOR. [*In wonder, looks up at her.*] And you do know

what you are doing. [*In understanding, takes her hand.*]
My dear—my very dear—

MADAME. I will go to Molly now. I won't leave her.
[*Straightens his hair.*] You need never worry about
me. Whether my way is good or not— [*Crossing R.*]
—it is my way.

MAYOR. [*Rises, catches her hand as she passes him.*]
Thank you, my dear, for telling me. [*He holds her for a
moment, then kisses her on the cheek.*]

MADAME. [*Looking down, touches a button on his coat.*]
You're going to lose this button. I'll sew it back tonight.
[*Exits R., closes door.*]

MAYOR. [*Turns toward door U.L., then back to* WINTER.]
Doctor, how do you think Molly looked?

WINTER. She'll be all right. Close to hysteria, I guess.
But she's good stock. Good strong stock. She'll be all
right.

LANSER. [*Comes in stiffly U.L. He has on a new pressed
uniform with a little dagger at the belt.*] Your Excellency. [*He glances at* WINTER.] Doctor. I'd like to speak
to you alone.

MAYOR. Doctor!

[LANSER *crosses U.R. above table.*]

WINTER. [*Rises, crosses L. front of table.*] Yes.

MAYOR. Will you come back to me this evening?

WINTER. Well, I have a patient—

MAYOR. I have a feeling I'll want you here with me.

WINTER. I'll be here. [*Crosses to doors U.L.*] I'll be here.
[*Closes doors after him, exits.*]

LANSER. [*Waits courteously. Watches door close. He
looks at table and chairs arranged about it, crosses to R.
end table.*] I'm very sorry about this. I wish it hadn't
happened. [MAYOR *faces away from* LANSER.] I like you,
and I respect you. I have a job to do. You surely recog-

nize that. [MAYOR *does not answer. At the end of each sentence* LANSER *waits for an answer, and none comes.*] We don't act on our own judgment. There are rules laid down for us. Rules made in the Capitol. This man has killed an officer.

ORDEN. [*Slowly turns to him.*] Why didn't you shoot him then? That was the time to do it.

LANSER. [*Crossing U.R.*] Even if I agreed with you, it would make no difference. You know as well as I that punishment is for the purpose of preventing other crimes. [*Crosses to table.*] Since it is for others, punishment must be publicized. It must even be dramatized. [MAYOR *turns away to his desk.*]

MAYOR. Yes—I know the theory—I wonder whether it works. [*Sits desk chair.*]

LANSER. Mayor Orden, you know our orders are inexorable. We must get the coal. If your people are not orderly, we will have to restore that order by force. [*His voice grows stern.*] We must shoot people if it is necessary. If you wish to save your people from hurt, you will help us to keep order. Now . . . [*Crossing to above table.*] . . . it is considered wise by my government that punishments emanate from the local authorities.

MAYOR. [*Softly, rises, crosses to chair L. of table.*] So . . . the people did know, they do know— [*Speaks louder.*] You wish me to pass sentence of death on Alexander Morden after a trial here?

LANSER. Yes. And you will prevent a great deal of bloodshed later if you will do it.

MAYOR. [*Pulls out the chair at L. end and sits down. He seems to be the judge and* LANSER *the culprit. He drums his fingers on table.*] You and your government do not understand. In all the world yours is the only government and people with a record of defeat after defeat for centuries, and always because you did not understand.

[*He pauses for a moment.*] This principle does not work. First, I am the Mayor. I have no right to pass sentence of death under our law. There is no one in this community with that right. If I should do it I would be breaking the law as much as you.

LANSER. Breaking the law?

MAYOR. You killed six men when you came in and you hurt others. Under our law you were guilty of murder, all of you. Why do you go into this nonsense of law, Colonel? There is no law between you and us. This is war. You destroyed the law when you came in, and a new cruel law took its place. You know you'll have to kill all of us or we in time will kill all of you.

LANSER. May I sit down?

MAYOR. Why do you ask? That's another lie. You could make *me* stand if you wanted.

LANSER. [*Seats himself R. end table.*] No . . . I respect you and your office, but what I think—I, a man of certain age and certain memories—is of no importance. I might agree with you, but that would change nothing. The military, the political pattern I work in, has certain tendencies and practices which are invariable.

MAYOR. And these tendencies and practices have been proven wrong in every single test since the beginning of the world.

LANSER. [*Laughing bitterly.*] I, a private man—with certain memories—might agree with you. Might even add that one of the tendencies of the military mind is an inability to learn. An inability to see beyond the killing which is its job. [*He straightens his shoulders.*] But I am not a private man. The coal miner must be shot . . . publicly, because the theory is that others will then restrain themselves from killing our men.

MAYOR. Then we needn't talk any more.

LANSER. Yes, we must talk. We want you to help.

MAYOR. [*Sits quietly for a moment, then looks up smiling.*] I'll tell you what I'll do. How many men were on the machine guns that killed our soldiers?

LANSER. About twenty.

MAYOR. Very well. If you will shoot them, I will usurp the power to condemn Morden.

LANSER. You are not serious?

MAYOR. I am serious.

LANSER. This can't be done, you know it. This is nonsense.

MAYOR. I know it. And what you ask can't be done. It is nonsense too.

LANSER. [*Sighing.*] I suppose I knew it. Maybe Corell will have to be Mayor after all. [*He looks up quickly.*] You'll stay for the trial?

MAYOR. [*With warmth.*] Yes, I'll stay. Then he won't be alone.

LANSER. [*Looks at him and smiles sadly.*] We've taken on a job, haven't we?

MAYOR. Yes. The one impossible job in the world. The one thing that can't be done.

LANSER. Yes?

MAYOR. To break man's spirit . . . permanently. [MAYOR's *head sinks a little toward table. The room is quite dark by now.*]

A SLOW CURTAIN

PART ONE

Scene IV

Scene: *It is a half hour later.*
The same as before. The room is fairly dark. The brackets in the little drawing-room are lighted. The room has been stripped of all its pictures, bric-a-brac and furniture, except the long dining-room table which is in the center, and 5 chairs around the table. 3 small chairs are standing against wall L. On the wall L. above where the MAYOR'S *desk stood, an iron bracket has been driven into the wall and a lighted gasoline lantern hangs. The court martial is in session.*

LANSER *sits above table C., with* HUNTER *on his R.* TONDER *stands at attention U.R.* LOFT, *with a little pile of papers in front of him, sits R. end table.* MAYOR *sits on* LANSER'S *L., and* PRACKLE *is at L. end table.* PRACKLE *is doodling with his pencil. Guarding the doors U.L. and facing the audience, two* GUARDS *stand with bayonets fixed, with helmets on their heads. Another* SOLDIER *stands at door D.L. They are wooden images. And between them stands* ALEX MORDEN, *a big young man with a wide, low forehead, deep-set eyes and a long sharp nose. His chin is firm, his mouth sensual and wide. He is a big man, broad of shoulder and narrow of hip. In front of him his manacled hands clasp and unclasp, and make a little clink of metal. He is dressed in black trousers, a blue shirt, a dark blue tie, and a dark coat shiny with wear.* LOFT *is standing at his end of table, beginning to read from a paper. He reads mechanically.*

LOFT. "When ordered back to work, he refused to go. And when the order was repeated, the prisoner attacked Captain Loft with a pickaxe. Captain Bentick interposed his body . . ."

MAYOR. Sit down, Alex. [LOFT *stops reading and glances at him.*] One of you guards get him a chair.

[*One of the* GUARDS *turns and hauls up a chair unquestioningly from wall L. to L.C.*]

LOFT. It is customary for the prisoner to stand.

MAYOR. Let him sit down. Only we will know. You can report that he stood.

LOFT. [*Stiffly.*] It is not customary to falsify reports.

MAYOR. Sit down, Alex. [ALEX *sits down and his manacled hands are restless.*]

LOFT. This is contrary to all . . .

LANSER. [*Looks up from writing, interrupting.*] Let him sit down.

LOFT. [*Clears throat and continues to read.*] "Captain Bentick interposed his body and received a blow on the head which crushed his skull." A medical report is appended. Does the Colonel wish me to read it?

LANSER. No need. Make it as short as you can.

LOFT. [*Reading.*] "These facts have been witnessed by several of our soldiers, whose statements are attached. This military court finds the prisoner guilty of murder and recommends the death sentence." Does the Colonel wish me to read the statements of the soldiers?

LANSER. [*Sighing.*] No. [LOFT *sits.* LANSER *turns to* ALEX.] You don't deny you killed the Captain, do you?

ALEX. [*Smiling sadly.*] I hit him. I don't know that I killed him. I didn't see him afterwards.

[MAYOR *and* ALEX *smile at each other.*]

LOFT. [*Rising.*] Does the prisoner mean to imply that Captain Bentick was killed by someone else?

ALEX. I don't know. I only hit him . . . and then somebody hit me.

LANSER. [*Wearily.*] Do you want to offer any explanation? I can't think of anything that will change the sentence, but we'll listen.

LOFT. [*Breaking in.*] I respectfully submit that the Colonel should not have said that. It indicates that the court is not impartial. [*Sits.*]

LANSER. [*Looks at* MAYOR, *then says to* ALEX.] Have you any explanation?

ALEX. [*Lifts right hand to gesture, and the manacle brings the left hand with it. He looks embarrassed and puts them into his lap again.*] I was mad, I guess. I have a pretty bad temper and when he said I had to go to work . . . I got mad and I hit him. I guess I hit him hard. It was the wrong man. [*He points at* LOFT.] That is the man I wanted to hit. That one.

LANSER. It doesn't matter who you wanted to hit. Anybody would have been the same. Are you sorry you did it? It would look well in the record if he were sorry.

[*Speaks aside to* LOFT *and* HUNTER.]

ALEX. [*Puzzled.*] Sorry? I'm not sorry. He told me to go to work. I'm a free man. I used to be Alderman. He said I had to work.

LANSER. But if the sentence is death, won't you be sorry then?

ALEX. [*Sinks his head and ponders honestly.*] No. You mean would I do it again?

LANSER. That's what I mean.

ALEX. [*Thoughtfully.*] I do not think I'm sorry.

LANSER. Put in the record that the prisoner is overcome with remorse. Sentence is automatic, you understand.

The court has no leeway. The court finds you guilty and
sentences you to be shot immediately. I do not see any
reason to torture you with this any more. Now, is there
anything I have forgotten?

MAYOR. You have forgotten me. [*He stands up, pushes
back his chair and steps over to* ALEX.] Alexander, I am
the Mayor . . . elected.

ALEX. I know it, sir. [*Starts to stand, but* MAYOR, *hand
on his shoulder, eases* ALEX *back into chair.*]

MAYOR. Alex, these men have taken our country by
treachery and force.

LOFT. [*Rising.*] Sir, this should not be permitted.

LANSER. [*Rising.*] Be silent. Is it better to hear it, or
would you rather it were whispered? [*Crosses U. to windows.*]

MAYOR. [*Continuing.*] When the enemy came, the people
were confused and I was confused. Yours was the first
clear act. Your private anger was the beginning of a
public anger. I know it is said in the town that I am acting with these men. I will show the town that I am
not. . . . But you . . . you are going to die. [*Softly.*]
I want you to know.

ALEX. [*Dropping his head and then raising it.*] I know
it. I know it, sir.

LANSER. [*Loudly, crossing to* LOFT.] Is the squad ready?

LOFT. [*Rising.*] Outside, sir.

LANSER. Who is commanding? [*Crossing to fireplace.*]

LOFT. Lieutenant Tonder, sir. [TONDER *raises his head,
and his chin is hard but his eyes are frightened.* LANSER
looks at his watch.]

MAYOR. [*Softly.*] Are you afraid, Alex?

ALEX. Yes, sir.

MAYOR. I can't tell you not to be. I would be, too. And so
would these . . . young gods of war.

LANSER. [*Facing table.*] Call your squad.

[OFFICERS *at the table rise, stand at attention.*]

TONDER. [*Crossing to* LANSER.] They're here, sir. [*Crosses L. to doors U.L., then* TWO SOLDIERS *step to* ALEX.]

MAYOR. Alex, go knowing that these men will have no rest . . . no rest at all until they are gone . . . or dead. You will make the people one. It's little enough gift to you, but it is so. . . . No rest at all. [ALEX *has shut his eyes tightly.* MAYOR *leans close and kisses him on the cheek.*] Goodbye, Alex. [*The* GUARDS *take* ALEX *by the arm and guide him. He keeps his eyes tightly closed. They guide him through the door between them. The* THIRD SOLDIER *and* TONDER *follow them out. The sound of the squad's feet in the passageway marches on wood and out of the house. The* MEN *about the table are silent. Outside the snow begins to fall.*] I hope you know what you are doing.

[LOFT *gathers his papers together. From outside come the commands* "Attention! Right Face! Forward March!" *and the* SOLDIERS' *footsteps are heard disappearing.*]

LANSER. In the Square, Captain?
LOFT. In the Square. It must be public.
MAYOR. I hope you know what you are doing.
LANSER. Man, whether we know it or not, it is what must be done.

[*A silence falls on the room and each man listens. After ten seconds, from the distance comes the commands:* "Ready! Aim! Fire!", *followed by the blast of a machine gun.* MAYOR *puts his hands to his forehead and fills his lungs deeply.* LOFT *and* HUNTER *sit at their places.* LANSER *crosses U. to his chair. As he reaches it, suddenly there is a shot outside. The glass of the window crashes inward.* PRACKLE *wheels about. He puts his hand to his shoulder.* HUNTER *and* LOFT *jump away from table and draw their revolvers.*]

LANSER. [*Sharply.*] Rigid! [OFFICERS *snap to attention;* LANSER, *to* PRACKLE.] Are you badly hurt?

PRACKLE. My shoulder.

LANSER. [*Crossing D. to table.*] Report to the hospital!

PRACKLE. Sir! [*Picks up helmet and coat, exits U.L.*]

LANSER. Captain Loft!

LOFT. Sir!

LANSER. Find the man who fired that shot.

LOFT. Sir! [*Picks up helmet and coat, exits U.L., running.*]

LANSER. [*To* LOFT *as he goes.*] There should be tracks in the snow. [*From outside the commands:* "Company attention! Left face! Double quick forward march!", *and the sound of running soldiers.*] Major Hunter, take Lieutenant Tonder and a detail. Search every house in the town for weapons. Shoot down any resistance. Take five hostages for execution.

HUNTER. Sir! [*Picks up helmet and coat, exits U.L.*]

LANSER. You, Mayor Orden, are in protective custody.

MAYOR. A man of certain memories.

LANSER. A man of no memories. We will shoot five—ten— a hundred for one! [*Crosses to window, then to L. end table.*] So it starts again.

MAYOR. [*Crossing to R. end table.*] It's beginning to snow.

LANSER. We'll have to have that glass fixed. The wind blows cold through a broken window.

MAYOR. Yes, the wind blows cold!

CURTAIN

PART TWO

Scene I

Time: *Two months later.*

Scene: *Still the downstairs room. It will be even more changed now. A kind of discomfort will have crept in. A slight mess due not to dirt so much as to the business of the men. It is very cold outside and not comfortably warm inside. Let the men wear coats and seem to be a little chilly all the time. This scene takes place at night. The blackout curtains are drawn tight. On the table, the same dining-room table, there are two gasoline lanterns which throw a hard white light.* [note: *These lanterns have to be pumped occasionally to keep the pressure up.*] *The light is cold and throws hard shadows. Also such a light from below will distort faces by throwing the light upward. On the table are several tin cups and plates. The room has been stripped bare of all drapes. Over the mantel hangs a map of the locality. Against the wall R. is a stack of duffle bags filled with equipment. More duffle-bags stand against the wall U.R. On this wall hangs a work drawing of* hunter's *rail line from the mine to the dock. A surveyor's sight on a tripod stands in a corner. At the windows U.C. on the table that was there in Scene I stands a Maxim machine gun pointing out the L. window. The cartridge belt is in place. Sandbags support the gun. On the wall U.L. hangs a bulletin board with a mail box. Against the L. wall where the* mayor's *desk stood there now is an army cot with pillow and blankets. On this wall upstage is a board with nails from which hang a Tommy gun, a duffle-bag, several greatcoats and helmets. Downstage on the wall*

*hangs another work drawing. From this wall, also, hangs
a newspaper-shaded lamp.*
Throughout the scene the sound of wind outside is heard.
AT RISE: HUNTER *is sitting at his drawing board at L.
end table, working with T-square and triangle.* PRACKLE
*sits in a straight chair, his feet up on another, in front
of a stove that has been set up front of the mantel, reading an illustrated paper. Behind the table* TONDER *is
writing a letter. He holds the pen pinched high, and occasionally looks up from his letter; looks at the ceiling
as though thinking, then nervously crumples the paper
he has been writing on, throws it away and starts his letter again.*

PRACKLE. [*Looking down at illustrated paper.*] I can
close my eyes and see every shop on this street here.
[HUNTER *goes on with his work and* TONDER *writes a few
words.*] There is a restaurant right behind here. You
can't see it in the picture, called Burden's.
HUNTER. [*Without looking up.*] I know the place. They
had good pastry.
PRACKLE. Do you remember those little poppyseed
cakes? Everything was good there. Not a single bad thing
did they serve, and their coffee . . .
TONDER. They won't be serving coffee now—or cakes.
PRACKLE. Well, I don't know about that. They did and
they will again, and there was a waitress there— [*He
looks down at magazine.*] She had the strangest eyes—
has, I mean—always kind of moist-looking as though
she had just been laughing or crying. [*He looks at ceiling and speaks softly.*] I was out with her. She was something. I wonder why I didn't go back oftener. I wonder
if she is still there.
TONDER. [*Gloomily.*] Probably not. Working in a factory, maybe.

PRACKLE. [*Laughing.*] I hope they aren't rationing girls at home.

TONDER. It'll probably come to that, too.

PRACKLE. [*Playfully turning to him.*] You don't care much for girls, do you? Not much you don't!

TONDER. [*Puts down his pen.*] I like them for what girls are for. I don't let them crawl around my other life.

PRACKLE. [*Tauntingly turns back to his magazine.*] Seems to me they crawl all over you all the time.

TONDER. [*Obviously to change the subject. Rises, pumps lantern on R. end table.*] I hate these damn lanterns. Major, when are you going to get that dynamo fixed?

HUNTER. Should be done by now. I have plenty of good men working on it and I'll double the guard on it from now on. [TONDER *crosses to lantern L. and pumps it.*]

PRACKLE. Did you get the fellow that wrecked it?

HUNTER. [*A little grimly.*] Might be any one of five men. I got all five! [TONDER *crosses to his chair, sits. Musingly.*] It's so damn easy to wreck a dynamo if you know how. Just short it and it wrecks itself. The light ought to be on any time now.

PRACKLE. [*Still looking at magazine.*] I wonder when we'll be relieved? I wonder when we can go home for awhile? [*Looking at him.*] Major, wouldn't you like to go home for a while?

HUNTER. [*Looks up from his work and his face is hopeless for a moment.*] Yes. Of course. [*He recovers himself.*] I've re-built this four times. [*He indicates drawing-board.*] I don't know why the bombs always choose this particular siding. I'm getting tired of this piece of track. Can't fill in the craters. The ground is frozen too hard.

[*The electric lights come on.* TONDER *reaches out and turns off gasoline lantern on table R.* HUNTER *turns off lantern near him.*]

TONDER. Thank God for that. These lights make me nervous. They're cold. [*He folds the letter he has been writing.*] I wonder why more letters don't come through? I've only had one in three weeks.

PRACKLE. Maybe she doesn't write to you.

TONDER. Maybe. [*He is nervous. Says to* HUNTER.] If anything happened—at home, I mean—do you think they'd let us know? Anything bad, I mean? Any deaths or things like that?

[*There is a light tap on door R. and* JOSEPH *comes in with a scuttle of coal. He moves silently through the room and sets scuttle down at stove so softly it makes no noise. He turns, without looking at anyone, and goes silently toward door.*]

PRACKLE. [*Loudly.*] Joseph! [JOSEPH *turns without replying and without looking up, and bows very slightly.*] Joseph, is there any wine, any brandy? [JOSEPH *shakes his head.*]

TONDER. [*Starts, his face wild with anger. Shouts.*] Answer, you swine! Answer in words!

JOSEPH. [*Does not look up; speaks tonelessly.*] No, sir. No, sir, there is no wine.

TONDER. [*Furiously.*] And no brandy?

JOSEPH. [*Looking down, speaks tonelessly again.*] There is no brandy, sir. [*He stands perfectly still.*]

[TONDER *crosses to mail-box, seals envelope, drops letter, turns back to his chair and sees* JOSEPH *still standing.*]

TONDER. What do you want?

JOSEPH. I want to go, sir.

TONDER. [*Furiously.*] Then go, God damn it!

[JOSEPH *turns and is about to leave the room.*]

HUNTER. Wait a minute. Is there some coffee?

JOSEPH. [*Pausing.*] Yes, sir.

HUNTER. Well, bring a pot of coffee. [JOSEPH *exits.* HUNTER *looks at* TONDER.] He had you shouting. That's what he wanted to do.

TONDER. [*Shakily.*] I'm all right. Sometimes they drive me a little crazy. You know they're always listening behind doors— [*Softly.*] I'd like to get out of this God-forsaken hole!

PRACKLE. [*Bitterly.*] Tonder was going to live here after the war. [*He imitates* TONDER's *voice.*] "Put four or five farms together. Make a nice place—kind of a family seat," wasn't it? Going to be a little Lord of the Valley, weren't you? "Nice, pleasant people—beautiful lawns and deer and little children." Isn't that the way it was, Tonder?

TONDER. [*As he speaks* TONDER's *head drops and he clasps his temples with his hands and speaks with emotion.*] Don't talk like that. These horrible people! They're cold! They never look at you, never speak. They answer like dead men. They obey. And the girls frozen —frozen.

[JOSEPH *enters with a large coffee-pot.*]

HUNTER. Put it down there. [*He puts it on table.*] That's all. [JOSEPH *exits silently.* PRACKLE *crosses to table, pours cup of coffee and takes it to* HUNTER.] Thanks.

[TONDER *pours himself cup of coffee.* PRACKLE *crosses back and pours one for himself.*]

TONDER. [*Tastes coffee, licks his lips.*] Does it taste all right to you?

HUNTER. [*Tasting.*] It isn't very good.

TONDER. But it's kind of bitter—not like coffee.

[PRACKLE *tastes his.* HUNTER *takes another drink.*]

HUNTER. [*Sharply.*] Now let's stop this nonsense. The coffee is good or it isn't. If it is good, drink it. If it isn't, don't drink it. [*Puts down his cup.*] Let's not have this questioning.

PRACKLE. [*Attempting to be light.*] I heard a funny thing the other day. Sergeant Mars told me he heard that a whole company in the South died from mushroom poisoning put in a stew. Five of my men got stomach-aches right away.

TONDER. [*Puts down his cup.*] We shouldn't let them handle anything we eat. They could put poison in everything.

HUNTER. You're just as bad as your men. You halfway believe what you're saying. [*Drinks from his coffee cup.* TONDER *crosses L. to cot bed, sits.*] It's just bad coffee—that's all. Bad, bitter coffee. [*Puts down cup.*]

PRACKLE. I hope so. [*Finishes his coffee. Rises, crosses to his chair D.R. Laughs as though he is saying a silly thing.*] God help us if they ever get top hand! [*Sits.*]

TONDER. [*Puts hands to his temples. Speaks brokenly.*] There's no rest from it day or night. [*His voice has a soft tenseness of controlled hysteria.*] No rest off duty. [*Breaks for a moment.*] I'd like to go home. I want to talk to a girl. There's a girl in this town. I see her all the time. I want to talk to that girl.

[*At that moment the lights go out again, leaving the stage in darkness.* HUNTER'S *voice speaks while he lights lanterns.*]

HUNTER. There they go again. [*Lights lantern L.*] Everybody in town seems to take a crack at my dynamo. [*Crosses to lantern R., lights it.*] You know, the other day a little boy shinnied up a pole and smashed a transformer. [*Crosses to his chair.*] What can you do with children? [*Crosses to* TONDER. *Speaks paternally to him.*] Tonder, do your talking to us, if you have to talk. There's nothing these people would like better than to know that your nerves are getting thin. [*Crosses to his chair, sits.*] Don't let the enemy hear you talk this way.

TONDER. That's it! The enemy—everywhere! Every man and woman. Even children. Waiting. The white faces behind the curtains, listening. We've beaten them. We've won everywhere and they wait and obey and they wait. Half the world is ours. Is it the same in other places, Major?

HUNTER. I don't know. [*Goes back to his work.*]

TONDER. That's it, we don't know. The reports—"everything under control, everything under control." Conquered countries cheer our soldiers. Cheer the New Order. [*His voice changes and grows softer.*] What do the reports say about us? Do they say we're cheered, loved, flowers in our paths?

HUNTER. [*As though to a child.*] Now that's off your chest, do you feel better?

[TONDER *rises, exits L.*]

PRACKLE. [*Miserably.*] He shouldn't talk that way. Let him keep things to himself. He's a soldier, isn't he? Let him be a soldier.

[*Door U.L. opens quietly and* LOFT *comes in. His nose is pinched and red. His great overcoat collar is high about his ears. He takes off his helmet and gloves, puts them on bed.*]

LOFT. I see they got your dynamo again. Your men ought to be more careful.

HUNTER. I heard you had a little trouble at the mine today.

LOFT. Well, I fixed that. [*Taking off his coat.*]

PRACKLE. What happened? [LOFT *turns sharply to him.*] Sir.

LOFT. [*Hangs his coat on nail U.L.*] Oh, the usual thing. The slow-down and a wrecked dumpcar. I saw the wrecker, though. Shot him. [*Crossing R.*] I have a cure for it now, though. Each man takes out a certain amount of coal. Can't starve the men or they can't work. But if the coal doesn't come out— [*Crosses to door R., closes it, then crosses to stove.*] —no food for the families. We'll have the men eat at the mine so there's no dividing at home. That will cure it. They work or their kids don't eat. I told them just now.

HUNTER. What did they say?

LOFT. [*Crossing to R. end table. His eyes narrow fiercely.*] Say? What do they ever say? Nothing. [*Bangs his fist on table.*] Nothing at all! Well, you'll see the coal come out now. [*Turns R. and stops short as he sees that the door he has just closed is open again. Turns to* HUNTER.] I thought I closed that tight.

HUNTER. You did.

[LOFT *quietly approaches door, draws his revolver, kicks door wide open and exits. At that moment* TONDER *enters from L., closes door after him.* LOFT *enters from R. and closes door. Crosses to* PRACKLE.]

PRACKLE. [*Turning pages of his illustrated paper again.*] Captain, have you seen these monster guns we were using in the East?

LOFT. Oh, yes. I've seen them fired. They are wonderful.

TONDER. [*Breaks in, crossing C. to front table.*] Captain, do you get much news from home?

LOFT. Yes—a certain amount.

TONDER. Is everything all right there?

LOFT. Wonderful. We move ahead everywhere.

TONDER. The British aren't defeated yet?

LOFT. They are defeated in every engagement.

TONDER. But they fight on?

LOFT. A few air raids, no more.

TONDER. And the Russians?

LOFT. It's all over.

TONDER. [*Insistently.*] But they fight on!

LOFT. A little skirmishing.

TONDER. Then we've just about won, Captain?

LOFT. [*Looks up at him.*] Yes.

TONDER. [*Looks closely at him.*] You believe this, don't you, Captain?

LOFT. [*Crossing toward* TONDER.] I don't know what you mean—?

TONDER. We'll be going home before long, then?

LOFT. Well, the reorganization will take a long time. The New Order can't be put into effect in a day.

TONDER. All our lives, perhaps?

HUNTER. Quiet, Tonder!

LOFT. [*Comes close to* TONDER.] Lieutenant, I don't like the tone of your questions. I don't like the tone of doubt.

[TONDER *turns away, crosses U.L.*]

HUNTER. [*Looking up.*] Don't be hard on him, Loft. He's tired. We're all tired.

LOFT. I'm tired, too, but I don't let doubt get in.

HUNTER. [*Irritably.*] Don't devil him. [LOFT *crosses to above table to pour cup of coffee.*] Where's the Colonel, do you know?

LOFT. Making his report. He's asking for reinforcements. [PRACKLE *and* TONDER *turn to look at him.*] It's a bigger job than we thought.

PRACKLE. [*Excitedly, rises, crosses to him.*] Will he get them?

LOFT. Of course.

TONDER. [*Smiles.*] Reinforcements. [*Softly.*] Or maybe replacements. [*Crossing above table to* LOFT.] Maybe we could go home for awhile. [*He is smiling.*] I could walk down the street and people would say "hello" and they'd like me.

PRACKLE. [*Crossing D.R.*] Don't start talking like that. [*Sits.*]

TONDER. There would be friends about and I could turn my back to a man without being afraid.

LOFT. [*Disgustedly.*] We've enough trouble without having the staff go crazy.

TONDER. [*Insistently.*] You really think replacements will come, Captain?

LOFT. Certainly. Look, Lieutenant, we've conquered half the world. We must police it for awhile.

TONDER. But the other half?

LOFT. It will fight on hopelessly for awhile.

TONDER. Then we must be spread out all over?

LOFT. For awhile.

TONDER. [*Breaking over.*] Maybe it will never be over. Maybe it can't be over. Maybe we've made some horrible mistake.

HUNTER. Shut up, Tonder!

LOFT. [*Rises. During this speech he has drawn himself up until he is a hard rigid thing, his jaw set and tight, his eyes squinted with intensity.*] Lieutenant—if you had said this outside this room, I should prefer a charge of treason against you. Treason not only against the Leader but against your race. Perhaps you are tired. That is no excuse. We are all tired, but we do not forget the destiny of our race. Make no mistake, Lieutenant, we shall conquer the world. We shall impose our faith and our strength on the world. And any weakness in ourselves we shall cut off. I will not bring the charge this time. But I will be watching you. Weakness is treason—do not forget it. [*Crosses L. to cot bed.*]

TONDER. [*Looking up at him.*] Weakness?

LOFT. [*As he sits.*] Weakness is treason!

TONDER. Weakness is treason? [*Sits in his chair above table.*]

PRACKLE. [*Nervously.*] Stop it! [*Rises, crosses to above stove. To* HUNTER.] Make him stop it!

TONDER. [*To himself.*] Treason?

HUNTER. Be quiet, Tonder!

TONDER. [*He speaks like a man a little out of his head. Laughingly, a little embarrassedly as he speaks.*] I had a funny dream. I guess a dream. Maybe it was a thought. Or a dream. [*Leans back in his chair.*]

PRACKLE. Stop it.

TONDER. Captain, is this place conquered?

LOFT. Of course.

TONDER. [*A little note of hysteria creeps into his laugh.*] Conquered, and we are afraid. Conquered, and we are surrounded. I had a dream. Out in the snow with the black shadows. And the cold faces in doorways. I had a thought. Or a dream.

[LOFT *rises.*]

PRACKLE. Stop it!

TONDER. I dreamed the Leader was crazy.

[HUNTER *laughs and is joined in the laughter by* LOFT *and* PRACKLE.]

HUNTER. [*Turns to* LOFT, *trying to make a joke of it.*] The Leader crazy!

LOFT. Crazy! The enemy have found out how crazy!

[*The laughter grows to a peak.*]

TONDER. [*Who has not stopped laughing.*] Conquest
after conquest! [HUNTER *stops laughing, then* LOFT *and*
PRACKLE *stop.*] Deeper and deeper into molasses. Maybe
the Leader's crazy. Flies conquer the fly-paper. Flies
capture two hundred miles of new fly-paper. [*His laughter is hysterical now.*]

LOFT. [*Gradually realizing the laughter is hysterical.
He steps close to* TONDER, *pulls him up out of his chair
and slaps him in the face.*] Lieutenant! Stop it! Stop it!

TONDER. [*The laughter stops. The stage is quiet.* TON-
DER *in amazement feels his bruised face with his hand. He
looks at his hand for a moment, sits in his chair, sob-
bing.*] I want to go home. [*His head sinks down on the
table.*]

CURTAIN

PART TWO

Scene II

Time: *Evening of the next day.*

Scene: *The living-room of* molly morden's *house. A pleasant, small room, rather poor and very comfortable. An arch R. leads to the kitchen. Downstage of this entrance stands an iron stove. On the floor beside it are a coal bucket, shovel, poker, a wood basket, and papers. Front of the stove is a straight chair facing into the room. Upstage of the kitchen entrance is another straight chair, and in the corner above this is a tall corner cabinet. Against the wall opposite the stove is an armless settee and a square table on which stands a brass oil lamp with a glass shade. Sewing-basket and materials, woolen cloth and a long scissors. The door to the passageway that leads to the outside is to the L. of settee. In the wall L. of this door is a window covered with blackout curtains. House plants stand on the window ledge. Under the window is a large chest. Rugs are on the floor. On shelves above the door L. and entrance R., and on the corner cabinet, stand a variety of decorative plates, pewter and copper utensils. The walls are papered in a warm blue with an old-fashioned fleur de lys design. On the walls are pictures. The light in the room is warm and soft.*

molly morden *is sitting alone on the settee beside the table. She is cutting the woolen material with the scissors. She is pretty and young and neat. Her golden hair is done on the top of her head, tied up with a blue bow. It is a quiet night. The wind whistles a little in the*

*chimney now and then. There is a little rustle at the door
and three sharp knocks. She puts down the material, goes
to the door and opens it and calls.*

MOLLY. Yes!
ANNIE [*Off.*] It's me—Annie.

[MOLLY *goes into storm passage.*]

MOLLY. Hello, Annie. I didn't expect you tonight.

[*A moment later a heavily-cloaked figure enters. This
is* ANNIE, *the cook, red-nosed, red-eyed and wrapped in
nondescript mufflers and a dark cap that covers her head.
She slips in quickly as though used to getting speedily
through doors and getting them closed behind her. She
stands sniffling her red nose and glancing quickly around
the room.*]

ANNIE. It's cold out, all right. The soldiers brought the
winter early. My father always said a war brought bad
weather, or bad weather brought a war. [MOLLY *enters,
having bolted outside door, and closes door.*] He didn't
know which.
MOLLY. [*Crossing to settee—places scissors on it.*] Take
off your things and come to the stove.
ANNIE. [*Importantly.*] No. I can't wait. *They're* coming!
MOLLY. [*Crossing to her.*] Who?
ANNIE. [*Sniffling.*] The Anders boys are sailing for England tonight. They got to. They're hiding now. The
Mayor wants to see them before they go.
MOLLY. What happened?
ANNIE. Their brother Jack was shot for wrecking a little
dump car. The soldiers are looking for the rest of the
family. Know how they do?
MOLLY. Yes, I know how they do.

ANNIE. [*Crosses to her. Holds out her hand. There is a little package in it.*] Here, take it. I stole it from the Colonel's plate. It's meat.

MOLLY. Thank you, Annie. Did you get some? [*Crosses R.*]

ANNIE. I cook it, don't I? I always get some. [*Crosses to stove, puts coal on fire.*]

MOLLY. [*Enters, crosses to settee, sits.*] Sit down, Annie, please, and stay awhile.

ANNIE. [*Crossing to door L.*] No time. I got to go back and tell the Mayor its all right here.

MOLLY. [*Rises, crosses L. to chest.*] It's an awful night to be sailing.

ANNIE. They're fishing men. [*Speaks simply.*] It's better than getting shot.

MOLLY. Yes, so it is. [*Sits on chest.*] How will the Mayor get out?

ANNIE. [*Laughs.*] Joseph is going to be in his bed in case they look in. Right in his night-shirt. Right next to Madame. [*She laughs again.*] Joseph better lie pretty quiet. [*Exit into hall.*]

MOLLY. [*Following her off.*] How soon are they coming?

ANNIE. [*Off.*] Maybe half. Maybe three-quarters of an hour. I'll come in first. Nobody bothers about me. [*She exits.*]

[MOLLY *bolts door, comes back into room, crosses to settee, picks up scissors. There is a knocking at outer door.*]

MOLLY. [*Crosses to door, calls.*] Annie! [*Knocking comes again. She goes into passage and we hear her voice.*] What do you want?

MAN'S VOICE. I come to— I don't mean any harm.

[MOLLY *enters room, followed by* TONDER. *She tries to close door on him, but he prevents it.*]

MOLLY. What do you want? You can't come in here.

TONDER. [*Dressed in his greatcoat.*] I don't mean any harm. Please let me come in.

MOLLY. [*Trying to close door on him.*] Get out!

TONDER. Miss, I only want to talk. That's all. I want to hear you talk. That's all I want.

MOLLY. I don't want to talk to you!

TONDER. Please, Miss. Just let me stay a little while. Then I'll go. Please. [MOLLY *releases door, crosses R.* TONDER *enters quickly and closes door. Trying to explain.*] Just for a little while couldn't we forget the war? Couldn't we talk together? Like people, together? Just for a little while?

MOLLY. [*Turns and looks at him.*] You don't know who I am, do you?

TONDER. I've seen you in the town. I know I want to talk to you.

MOLLY. [*He stands like a child looking very clumsy, as she says very softly.*] Why, you are lonely. [*Crosses to stove.*] It's as simple as that.

TONDER. [*Crossing to settee. Speaks eagerly.*] That's it. You understand. I knew you would. [*The words come tumbling out of him.*] I am lonely to the point of illness. It's nice here. It's warm. Can't I stay, please? [*He starts to unbutton his coat, but stops as she continues.*]

MOLLY. You can stay for a moment.

[*He crosses to chest and puts down his helmet. She looks at the stove. The house creaks. He becomes tense.*]

TONDER. [*Tense.*] Is someone here?

MOLLY. [*Crossing to chair front stove.*] No. The snow is heavy on the roof. [*Sits looking at him.*] I have no man any more to push it down.

TONDER. [*Gently.*] Did—was it something we did?

MOLLY. Yes.

TONDER. I'm sorry. [*He pauses for a moment.*] I wish I could do something. [*Crosses to settee—sits.*] I'll have the snow pushed off the roof, first thing in the morning.

MOLLY. No.

TONDER. [*Eagerly.*] Why not?

MOLLY. The people wouldn't trust me any more.

TONDER. I see. You *all* hate us. But I'd like to help you if you'll let me.

MOLLY. [*Rises. She is in control now. Her eyes narrow a little cruelly.*] Why do you ask? You are the conqueror. Your men don't *ask*. [*Crossing U.R.*] They *take* what they want.

TONDER. [*Rises, crosses to her.*] No. That's not what I want. That's not the way I want it.

MOLLY. [*Turns to him. Cruelly.*] You want me to like you, don't you, Lieutenant?

TONDER. [*Simply.*] Yes. You are so beautiful. So warm. [*She crosses to settee.*] I've seen no kindness in a woman's face for so long.

MOLLY. [*Turns to him.*] Do you see any in mine?

TONDER. [*Looking closely at her.*] I want to.

MOLLY. [*She drops her eyes at last. Sits sofa.*] You are making love to me, aren't you, Lieutenant?

TONDER. [*Sits chair, front of stove. Clumsily.*] I want you to like me. Surely I want you to like me. I want to see it in your eyes. I've watched you in the street. I've even given orders you must not be molested. Have you been molested?

MOLLY. [*Quietly.*] No, I've not been molested.

TONDER. They told us the people would like us here. Would admire us. And they don't. They only hate us. [MOLLY *rises, crosses L. He changes the subject as though working against time.*] You are so beautiful.

MOLLY. [*Turns to him.*] You are beginning to make love to me, Lieutenant. You must go soon.

TONDER. [*Rises, crosses C.*] A man needs love. A man dies without love. [MOLLY *crosses to chest.*] His insides shrivel, and his chest feels like a dry chip. I'm lonely.

MOLLY. [*Looking away from him.*] You'll want to go to bed with me, Lieutenant.

TONDER. I didn't say that. Why do you talk that way?

MOLLY. [*Turns to him, cruelly.*] Maybe I am trying to disgust you! I was married once. My husband is dead. [*Sits on chest. Her voice is bitter.*]

TONDER. I only want you to like me.

MOLLY. I know. You are a civilized man. You know that love-making is more full and whole and delightful if there is liking, too.

TONDER. Don't talk that way. [*Turns away, sits on settee.*]

MOLLY. [*Rises, crosses to him.*] We are a conquered people, Lieutenant. I am hungry. I will like you better if you feed me. My price is two sausages.

TONDER. You fooled me for a moment. But *you* hate me, too.

MOLLY. [*Crossing to chest.*] No. I don't hate you. I'm hungry. And— [*Turns to him.*] I hate you!

TONDER. I'll give you anything you need, but—

MOLLY. [*Interrupting.*] You want to call it something else? You don't want a whore. . . . Is that what you mean?

TONDER. [*Crosses to chair R., sits.*] I don't know what I mean! You make it sound full of hatred.

MOLLY. It's not nice to be hungry. Two sausages can be the most precious things in the world.

TONDER. [*Pleadingly.*] Don't say these things. Please don't.

MOLLY. Why not? [*Turns away to door.*] It's true.

TONDER. [*Rises, crosses C.*] It is not true. This can't be **true.**

MOLLY. It isn't true. I don't hate you. I am lonely. [TON-DER *sits on settee.* MOLLY *leans against door.*] The snow is heavy on the roof.

TONDER. [*Takes her hand. Places it to his cheek.*] Don't hate me. I'm only a soldier. I didn't ask to come here. You didn't ask to be my enemy. I am only a man, not a conquering man.

MOLLY. [*Stroking his head.*] I know.

TONDER. We have some little right to life.

MOLLY. [*Puts her cheek on his head.*] Yes. [*She leans a little toward him.*]

TONDER. I'll take care of you. We have some right to life in all the killing. [*She slowly straightens up. Suddenly she grows rigid, her eyes wide and staring as though she sees a vision. She draws away her hands sharply and crosses R.*] What is it? What's the matter. [*Her eyes stare straight ahead.*] What have I done?

MOLLY. [*In a haunted voice—facing away from him.*] I dressed him in his best clothes like a little boy for his first day of school. I buttoned his shirt and tried to comfort him. But he was beyond comfort. [*Sits chair front of stove.*] And he was afraid.

TONDER. [*Rises.*] What are you saying?

MOLLY. [*Stares right ahead and seems to see what she is describing.*] I don't know why they let him come home. He didn't know what was happening. He didn't even kiss me when he went. He was afraid. And very brave. Like a little boy on his first day at school.

TONDER. That was your husband.

MOLLY. And then—he marched away—not very well nor steadily, and you took him out—and shot him. It was more strange than terrible then. I didn't quite believe it then.

TONDER. Your husband?

MOLLY. Yes, my husband. And now in the quiet house I

believe it. Now with the heavy snow on the roof I believe it. And in the loneliness before day-break, in the
half-warmed bed, I know it then.

TONDER. [*He crosses to chest, picks up helmet, his face
full of misery.*] Good night. [*Crosses to door, puts on
helmet, turns to her.*] May I come back?

MOLLY [*Staring at the memory.*] I don't know.

TONDER. Please let me come back.

MOLLY. [*Rises, crosses U.C. to table.*] No.

[TONDER *looks at her for a moment and then goes quietly
out the door.* MOLLY *crosses to settee, sits. Very silently*
ANNIE *enters from kitchen R.*]

ANNIE. There was a soldier here.

MOLLY. Yes, Annie.

ANNIE. [*Suspiciously.*] What was he doing here?

MOLLY. [*Her voice dreaming.*] He came to make love
to me.

ANNIE. [*Crossing to her.*] Miss. What are you doing?
You haven't joined them, have you? You aren't with
them, like Corell?

MOLLY. [*Shaking her head.*] No. I'm not with them,
Annie.

ANNIE. If he comes back while the Mayor's here it will
'be your fault.

MOLLY. He won't come back.

ANNIE. [*Very suspiciously.*] Shall I tell them to come in
now? They're out behind the fence.

MOLLY. Yes. Tell them to come in.

[ANNIE *exits L., leaving door open.* MOLLY *rises, crosses
to chair R.* MOLLY *gets up. Shakes her head and tries to
get alive again. There is a little sound in the passage and
two tall blonde young men enter. They are dressed in*

pea-jackets and dark turtle-neck sweaters. They have stocking caps perched on their heads. They are wind-burned and strong and they look almost like twins. One is WILL ANDERS, *and the other* TOM ANDERS.]

WILL. [*Crossing R. takes off hat and gloves.*] Good evening, Molly. You heard?

[TOM *enters, crosses to settee.*]

MOLLY. Annie told me. It's a bad night to go.

TOM. [*Takes off hat.*] Better than a clear night. The planes see you on a clear night. What's the Mayor want, Molly?

MOLLY. I don't know. I heard about your brother. I'm sorry.

[*The two are silent. They look embarrassed.*]

TOM. Well, you know how it is, better than most.

MOLLY. Yes. I know.

[*Enter* MAYOR. *He wears a fur-lined coat, hat, and gloves.*]

MAYOR. [*Calls to* ANNIE.] Stand in the passage, Annie. Give us one knock for the patrol and one when it's gone. [*He closes door.*]

ANNIE. [*Off.*] Yes, sir.

MAYOR. Good evening, Molly.

MOLLY. [*Crossing to him to take his hat.*] Good evening Your Excellency. [*Takes hat to chest.*]

MAYOR. I got word you boys were going tonight.

[MOLLY *comes to him for his gloves, takes them to chest.*]

TOM. We have to go.

MAYOR. [*Nodding.*] Yes, I know.

TOM. [*Turns to* MAYOR.] You wanted to see us, sir?
MAYOR. [*Crossing to stove.*] Yes. I want to talk to you.
I have a plan. Dr. Winter and I have discussed it.

[*A sharp knock on door. The room is silent. Every eye
is turned toward the door.* TOM *crosses to window.* WILL
*steps toward door. Then first faintly, and growing
louder, comes the tramp of the patrol. They near the
door and their steps disappear in the distance. There is
a second tap on the door. Those in the room relax.*]

WILL. We haven't much time, sir.
MAYOR. [*Begins slowly.*] What I have to say won't take
long. I want to speak simply. This is a little town. Justice and injustice are in terms of little things. The people are angry and they have no way to fight back. Our
spirits and bodies aren't enough.
TOM. What can we do, sir?
MAYOR. We want to fight them and we can't. They are
using hunger on the people now. Hunger brings weakness. You boys are sailing for England. Tell them to
give us weapons.

[*Again there is a quick knock on the door and the people freeze where they are. The patrol comes by at double
step.* WILL *moves to the window.* TOM *goes into passageway. The running steps come abreast of the house. There
are muffled orders.*]

SOLDIER. Break ranks!
SOLDIER. This way!
SOLDIER. Over here!

[*And the patrol runs on by. There is a second tap on
the door.*]

MOLLY. They must be after someone.

[*Two rifle shots are heard in the distance.*]

WILL. I wonder if it's us?

TOM. [*Enters, uneasily to* WILL.] We should be going. [*To* MAYOR.] Do you want guns, sir? Shall we ask for guns?

MAYOR. No. Tell them how it is. We are watched. Any move we make calls for reprisal. If we could have simple weapons, secret weapons. Weapons of stealth. Explosives. Dynamite to blow out rails. Grenades if possible. Even poison. [*He speaks angrily—crossing R.*] This is no honorable war. This is a war of treachery and murder. Let us use the methods they have used on us. Let the British bombers drop their great bombs on the works, but let them also drop little bombs for us to use. To hide. To slip under rails. Under trucks. Then we will be secretly armed, and the invader will never know which of us is armed. Let the bombers bring us simple weapons. We'll know how to use them. [*Crosses D.R.*]

[MOLLY *sits on settee.*]

WILL. I've heard that in England there are still men in power who do not dare to put weapons in the hands of common people.

MAYOR. Oh. [*As though the wind had been knocked out of him.*] I hadn't thought of that. Well, we can only see. If such people still govern England and America, the world is lost anyway. Tell them what we say if they will listen. We must have help. But if we get it— [*His face grows hard.*] we will help ourselves. Then the invader can never rest again, never. We will blow up his supplies. [*Fiercely.*] We will fight his rest and his sleep. We will fight his nerves and his certainties.

TOM. If we get through, we'll tell them. Is that all, sir?

MAYOR. Yes, that's the core of it. [*Sits chair front stove.*]

TOM. What if they won't listen?

MAYOR. We can only try as you are trying the sea to-night.

[*The door opens and* ANNIE *comes in quickly.*]

ANNIE. There's a soldier coming up the path. [*She looks suspiciously at* MOLLY. MOLLY *rises. The others look at* MOLLY.] I locked the door.

[*There is a gentle knocking on outside door.*]

MAYOR. [*Rises in wonder.*] Molly, what is this? Are you in trouble?

MOLLY. No— No. Go out the back way. You can get out through the back. Hurry. [*She moves to entrance R.*]

[TOM *and* WILL *hurry out R. through kitchen.* ANNIE *crosses to chest for* MAYOR's *hat and gloves, takes them to him. He crosses to entrance, then turns to* MOLLY.]

MAYOR. Do you want me to stay, Molly?
MOLLY. No. It will be all right.

[MAYOR *exits.*]

ANNIE. [*Cold with suspicion.*] It's the same soldier.
MOLLY. [*Crosses D.R.*] Yes.
ANNIE. What's he want?
MOLLY. [*Crossing C.*] I don't know.
ANNIE. Are you going to tell him anything?
MOLLY. [*Wonderingly.*] No. [*Then sharply turning to her.*] No!
ANNIE. [*Quietly.*] Good night, then. [*Crosses to entrance R.*]
MOLLY. [*Crossing to front settee.*] Good night, Annie. Don't worry about me. [*Crosses to* ANNIE.]
ANNIE. Good night. [*Exits.*]

[MOLLY *stands watching her off. The knocking comes*

again. She crosses to settee. The knocking is repeated. She turns sharply and sits on settee. Her hand falls on the scissors she left on the settee earlier. She picks them up and looks at them intently. Again the knocking comes. She rises and places the scissors in her hand, dagger fashion. Then turns to lamp on table, turns it low and the room becomes nearly dark. The knocking is repeated. She crosses to door, throws it open.]

MOLLY. [*Her voice is stricken.*] I'm coming, Lieutenant —I'm coming.

CURTAIN

PART TWO

Scene III

Time: *Three weeks later. It is morning.*
Scene: *Living-room of the Palace of the* MAYOR. *The dining-table remains as it was placed the day* MORDEN *was shot. The room has become austere. It has lost the grace it had. And the comfort. Chairs are about the table, leaving the walls looking blank, and on the table a few papers are scattered, making it look like a business office.*
The armchair used at the beginning of the play is now in front of the stove. A card table is against wall L. in place of the cot bed. 3 chairs are around it. Empty beer bottles, tin cups, cigarette butts, and playing cards are on the table. The table C. has a chair at each end and one in the center above table. The blackout curtains are open. Otherwise the room is as we last saw it.
It is a dark day, overcast with clouds.
At Rise: *As the curtain goes up,* ANNIE *comes out of the* MAYOR's *room left. And on the way to the other entrance she swoops by the table looking at the papers that lie there. The door U.L. opens.* LOFT *comes in. He sees* ANNIE.

LOFT. [*Crossing to table.*] What are you doing here?
ANNIE. [*Sullenly.*] Yes, sir. [*Crosses to R. end table.*]
LOFT. [*Crossing to above table.*] I said, what are you doing here?

[SOLDIER *enters U.L., stands at door awaiting orders.*]
82

ANNIE. I thought to clean up, sir.

LOFT. Let things alone and go along.

ANNIE. Yes, sir. [*She exits quickly out of door R.*]

[LOFT *takes off helmet. A* SOLDIER *standing at door holds a number of blue packages, to the ends of which dangle strings and little pieces of cloth.*]

LOFT. Put them on the table. [*The* SOLDIER *gingerly lays packages on table.*] That's all.

[*The* SOLDIER *wheels and leaves the room.* LOFT *goes to front of table and picks up one of the packages. His face wears a look of distaste. He holds up the little cloth attached to the package. Holds it above his head and drops it. The cloth opens to a tiny parachute. And the package floats to the floor.* LOFT *picks up package and examines it.*]

LANSER. [*Coming quickly into the room, carrying a blue paper, followed by* HUNTER, *who has a square of yellow paper in his hand.* LANSER, *in a business-like tone.*] Good morning, Captain. [*He goes to chair C. above table and sits down. For a moment he looks at the little pile of packages, then picks one up and holds it. Speaks curtly.*] Have you examined these?

HUNTER. [*Pulls out chair L. end table and sits down. He looks at the yellow paper in his hand.*] Not very carefully. There are three breaks in the railroad, all within ten miles.

[LOFT *crosses to R. end table, takes off coat, puts it on chair.*]

LANSER. Well, take a look at them and see what you think of them.

HUNTER. [*Reaches for a package, strips off outer blue cover. Inside there are two items, a tube and a square package.* HUNTER *takes out his knife and cuts into tube.* LOFT *looks over his shoulder.* HUNTER *smells the cut place. Feels the material and rubs it between his two fingers.*] It's silly. It's commercial dynamite. I don't know what percent nitroglycerine until I test it. [*He looks at end of tube. It has an ordinary dynamite cap, fulminate mercury, and about a one-minute fuse. He tosses the tube on table.*] Very cheap. Very simple.

LANSER. [*Looking at* LOFT.] How many do you think were dropped?

LOFT. I don't know, sir. We picked up about fifty. But we found ninety more parachutes with nothing on them. The people must have hidden those packages.

LANSER. It doesn't really matter. They can drop as many as they want. We can't stop it. And we can't use it back against them. They haven't conquered anybody.

LOFT. [*Crosses to chair R. end table.*] We can beat them off the face of the earth. [*Sits.*]

[HUNTER *is prying copper cap out of the top of one of the sticks.*]

LANSER. Yes, we can do that. Have you looked at this wrapper, Hunter?

HUNTER. Not yet. I haven't had time.

LANSER. [*Quietly.*] Well, I have. It's kind of devilish, this thing. The wrapper is blue so it is easy to see. Take off the outer paper and here— [*He picks up smaller package and unwraps it.*]—Here is a piece of chocolate. Everybody will be looking for these things. Even our own soldiers will steal the chocolate. Children'll be looking for them like Easter eggs. [*A* SOLDIER *comes in U.L. and lays a square of yellow paper in front of* LANSER.] That's all. [SOLDIER *exits U.L.* LANSER *glances at it and laughs harshly.*] Here is something for you, Hunter. Two more breaks in your line.

LOFT. Did they drop them everywhere?

LANSER. Now that's the funny thing. I've talked to the Capitol. This is the only place they dropped them.

HUNTER. What do you make of that?

LANSER. Well, it's hard to say. I think this might be a test. If it works here they'll use it all over. And if it doesn't work here, they won't bother.

LOFT. Well, what are we going to do?

LANSER. I have orders to stamp this out so ruthlessly that it will stop right here.

HUNTER. How am I going to mend five breaks in a railroad? I haven't rails enough.

LANSER. Rip out some old siding.

HUNTER. That'll make a hell of a road-bed. [HUNTER *tosses the tube he has torn apart on the pile.*]

LOFT. We must stop this thing at once, sir. We must arrest and punish the people who pick these things up. We must get busy so that they won't think we are weak.

LANSER. [*Smiling at him.*] Take it easy. Let's see what we have first and then we'll think of remedies. [*He takes a new package from pile and unwraps it. He unwraps the chocolate and tastes it.*] This is a devilish thing. Good chocolate, too. I can't even resist it myself. The prize in the grab-bag. [*He picks up the dynamite.*] How effective is this, Hunter?

HUNTER. Very effective for small jobs. Dynamite with a cap and a one-minute fuse. Good if you know how to use it. No good if you don't.

LANSER. [*He is studying the print on inside of wrapper.*] Listen to this. They'll know how to use it— [*Reading from paper.*] "To the Unconquered People. Hide this. Do not expose yourself. Do not try to do large things with it." [*He begins to skip through.*] Now here: "Rails in the country—work at night—tie up transportation." Now here—instructions: "Rails. Place stick under rail, close to joint and tight against tie. Pack mud or hard-packed snow around it so that it is firm. When fuse is lighted, you have a slow count of sixty before it explodes." [LANSER *looks up at* HUNTER.]

HUNTER. It works.

LANSER. [*Looks back at his paper and skips through.*] "Bridges: Weaken but do not destroy." And here— "Transmission poles." And here: "Culverts—trucks." [*He lays paper down.*] Well, there it is.

LOFT. [*Angrily.*] We must do something. There must be a way to control this. What does Headquarters say?

LANSER. [*Purses his lips and his fingers play with one of the tubes.*] I could have told you what they would say before they said it. I have the order. "Set booby traps. Poison the chocolate." [*He pauses for a moment. Rises, crosses R. to stove.*] Hunter, I am a good loyal man, but sometimes when I hear the brilliant ideas of Headquarters, I wish I were a civilian. An old crippled civilian. The leaders always think they're dealing with stupid people. I don't say that this is the measure of their intelligence—do I?

HUNTER. [*Looking amused.*] Do you?

[LOFT *looks up at* LANSER.]

LANSER. [*Sharply.*] No. I don't. [*Crossing to front of table.*] But what will happen? One man will pick one of these and get blown to bits by our booby trap. One kid will eat chocolate and die of strychnine poisoning. And then— [*He looks down at his hands.*]—they'll poke them with poles or lasso them before they touch them. They'll try the chocolate on the cat. God damn it! [*Sits against table.*] These are intelligent people. Stupid traps won't catch them twice.

HUNTER. Why do you suppose it was only dropped here?

LANSER. For one of two reasons. [*Crossing to card table.*] Either this town was picked at random. Or else there is communication between this town and the outside. We know that some of the young men have got away.

LOFT. [*Rises. Repeating.*] We must do something. [*Slaps table.*]

LANSER. [*Angrily. He picks up some of the cards and shuffles them.*] Loft, I think I'll recommend you for the General Staff. You want to get to work before you even know what the problem is. This is a new kind of conquest. Always before it was possible to disarm people and keep them in ignorance. Now they listen to their radios and we can't stop them. [*He sits astraddle chair R. of table facing* LOFT.] They read handbills. Weapons drop from the sky for them. Now it's dynamite. Soon grenades. Then poison.

LOFT. [*Anxiously, rises, crosses C. front of table.*] They haven't dropped poison.

LANSER. [*Folding a card into a dart.*] No, but they will. Can you think what would happen to the morale of our men, or even to you, if the people had some of those little game darts? The points coated with cyanide. Silent deadly things. [*Throws card dart at* LOFT, *who steps back.*] What if you knew arsenic was about? Would you eat or drink comfortably?

HUNTER. [*Dryly.*] Are you writing the enemy's campaign?

LANSER. I am trying to anticipate it.

LOFT. We sit here talking. [*Crossing R.C.*] We should be looking for this dynamite. If there's organization among these people we have to find it, [*Crosses to R. end above table.*] and stamp it out.

LANSER. Yes. [*Rises, throws cards on table.*] We have to stamp it out, ferociously. [*Crosses R. to armchair.*] You take a detail, Loft. Get Prackle to take one. I wish we had more Junior officers. I wish we hadn't lost Tonder. [*Sits armchair.*]

LOFT. I don't like the way Lieutenant Prackle is acting, sir.

LANSER. What's he doing?

LOFT. [*Putting on his coat.*] Well, he's nervous and irritable. He's not himself at all.

LANSER. Yes, I know. That's the thing I talked about so much. [*He chuckles.*] I might have been a Major-General if I hadn't talked about it so much. We trained our young men for victory. They are glorious in victory. They don't know how to act in defeat. We told them they were brighter and braver than other young men. It's a shock to them to find that they aren't a bit brighter or braver than other young men.

LOFT. [*Crosses to* LANSER. *Harshly.*] What do you mean, defeat? We aren't defeated. [LANSER *looks coldly at him for a long moment. He doesn't speak, and finally* LOFT's *eyes waver.*] Sir!

LANSER. Thank you.

LOFT. You don't demand it of the others, sir.

LANSER. They don't think about it, so it isn't an insult. When you leave it out it is insulting.

LOFT. Yes, sir.

LANSER. Go now. Start your search. [LOFT *crosses to table, picks up helmet. Crosses L.C.* LANSER *rises.*] I don't want any shooting unless there's an overt act. You understand?

LOFT. Yes, sir. [*Salutes formally and goes out of the room U.L.*]

[LANSER *crosses U.R. to windows.*]

HUNTER. You were a little rough on him.

LANSER. Had to be. [*Crosses to table—picks up piece of*

dynamite.] He's frightened. I know his kind. He has to be disciplined when he is afraid or he will go to pieces. He relies on discipline the way other men rely on sympathy. I suppose you'd better get to your rails. To-night's the time when they'll really blow them. [*Sits chair above table.*]

HUNTER. Yes. [*Rises, crosses to door U.L.*] I suppose the orders are coming from the Capitol?

LANSER. Yes.

HUNTER. [*Crossing back to him.*] Are they—?

LANSER. You know what they are. Take the leaders. Shoot the leaders. Take hostages. Shoot the hostages. Take more hostages. Shoot them. [*His voice has risen and now it sinks almost to a whisper.*] And the hatred growing. And the hurt between us deeper and deeper.

HUNTER. [*Quietly.*] Colonel, do you want me to recommend—maybe you are overtired, Colonel? Could I say you are overtired?

LANSER. [*Covers his eyes with his hands for a moment. Then his shoulders straighten and his face grows hard.*] I'm not a civilian, Hunter. We are short enough of officers already. You know that. Get to your work, Major.

HUNTER. [*Clicks heels.*] Sir. [*He goes out the door and says*] Yes. He's in there.

PRACKLE. [*Comes in, carrying helmet, crosses to chair L. of table. His face sullen and belligerent.*] Colonel Lanser, sir. I wish to——

LANSER. Sit down. Sit down. [PRACKLE *sits chair L. of table, puts helmet on table.*] Rest a moment. Be a good soldier, Lieutenant.

PRACKLE. [*The stiffness goes out of him. He sits down heavily.*] I wish——

LANSER. Don't talk for a moment. I know what it is. You didn't think it would be this way.

PRACKLE. [*Rises, Crosses to R. end table.*] They hate us. They hate us so.

LANSER. [*Smiling wryly.*] I wonder if I know what it is. [PRACKLE *turns to him.*] It takes young men to make good soldiers. Young men need young women, is that it? [*Kindly.*] Does she hate you?

PRACKLE. [*Looks at him in amazement.*] I don't know, sir. [*Turns away.*] Sometimes she's only sorry.

LANSER. And you're pretty miserable.

PRACKLE. [*Crosses to chair R. of table, sits.*] I don't like it here, sir.

LANSER. No. You thought it would be fun. Lieutenant Tonder went to pieces. And then he went out and got himself killed. I could send you home. Do you want to be sent home, knowing we need you here?

PRACKLE. [*Uneasily.*] No, sir.

LANSER. [*Rises, crosses around to front of table, leans against table.*] Good. Now I'll tell you. And I hope you'll understand. You're not a man any more. You're a soldier. Your comfort is of no importance and your life not very much. If you live you will have memories. That's about all you will have. You must take orders and carry them out. Most of them will be unpleasant. But that's not your business. I will not lie to you, Lieutenant. They should have trained you for this. Not for cheers and flowers. [*His voice hardens; he gets to his feet.*] But you took the job. Will you stay with it, or quit it? We cannot take care of your soul.

PRACKLE. [*Stands up.*] Thank you, sir.

SOLDIER. [*Enters U.L.*] Mr. Corell to see you, sir.

LANSER. Send him in. [SOLDIER *exits.* LANSER *crosses around to above table.*] And the girl, Lieutenant. You may rape her or protect her or marry her. That is of no importance, as long as you shoot her when it is ordered. You may go now.

[PRACKLE *crosses L., picks up helmet, exits.* LANSER *sits and busies himself with his work.* CORELL *enters. But he is a changed man. And his expression is no longer jovial nor friendly. His face is sharp and bitter; he carries his hat and coat, puts them on chair L. of table.*]

CORELL. I should have come before, Colonel, but your lack of cooperation made me hesitant.

LANSER. Cooperation? You were waiting for a reply to your private report to the Capitol, I remember.

CORELL. [*Crossing around to above table L. of* LANSER.] I was waiting for much more than that. You refused me a position of authority. You said I was valueless. You did not realize that I was in this town long before you were. You left the Mayor in his office, contrary to my advice.

LANSER. Without him there might have been more disorder than there has been.

CORELL. That's a matter of opinion. This man is the leader of a rebellious people.

LANSER. He's just a simple man.

CORELL. You forget, Colonel, that I had my sources. Mayor Orden has been in constant contact with every happening in this community. On the night when Lieutenant Tonder was murdered, he was in the house where the murder was committed. When the girl escaped to the hills she stayed with one of his relatives. I traced her there but she was gone. When men have escaped, Orden has known about it and helped. I strongly suspect that he is in back of these little parachutes.

LANSER. [*Eagerly.*] But you can't prove it.

CORELL. The first things I know. The last I can't prove yet. Perhaps now you'll be willing to listen to me.

LANSER. [*Quietly.*] What do you suggest?

CORELL. These suggestions are a little stronger than

suggestions, Colonel. Orden must now be a hostage. And his life must depend on the peacefulness of this community. His life must depend on the lighting of one single fuse. [*Reaches into pocket and brings out a little folding book such as is used for identification. He flips it open and lays it in front of* LANSER.] This was the answer to my report, sir.

LANSER. [*Looks at book and speaks quietly.*] Um—you really did go over my head, didn't you? [*He looks up at* CORELL *with frank dislike in his eyes.*]

CORELL. Now, Colonel, must I suggest more strongly than I have that Mayor Orden must be held hostage?

LANSER. He's here. He hasn't escaped. [*Rises, crosses to R. end table.*] How can we hold him more hostage than we are?

[*In the distance there is an explosion, and both men look around in the direction from which it comes.*]

CORELL. [*A step to him.*] There it is. If this experiment succeeds, there will be dynamite in every conquered country.

LANSER. [*Quietly.*] What do you suggest?

CORELL. Orden must be held against rebellion.

LANSER. And if rebellion comes and we shoot Orden?

CORELL. Then that doctor's next. He's the next in authority.

LANSER. He holds no office. Well, suppose we shoot him— What then?

CORELL. Then rebellion is broken before it starts.

LANSER. [*Shakes his head a little sadly.*] Have you ever thought that one execution makes a hundred active enemies where we have passive enemies? Even patriotism is not as sharp as personal hurt, personal loss. A dead brother, a dead father—that really arms an enemy.

CORELL. [*Almost as though he had grounds for blackmail now.*] Your attitude, sir, may lead you to trouble. It is fortunate that I am—your friend.

LANSER. [*Crosses R. to arm chair; with a little contempt in his voice.*] I can see your report almost as though it were in front of me—

CORELL. [*Quickly.*] Oh! But you're mistaken, sir. I haven't—

LANSER. [*Turns to him.*] This war should be for the very young. They would have the proper spirit, but unfortunately they are not able to move guns and men about. I suffer from civilization. That means I can know one thing and do another. I know we have failed—I knew we would before we started. The thing the leader wanted to do cannot be done.

CORELL. [*Excitedly, leaning toward him across table.*] What is this? What do you say?

LANSER. [*Quietly, crosses to R. end of table.*] Oh! Don't worry. I will go about it as though it could be done and do a better job than the zealots could. And when the tide turns, I may save a few lives, from knowing how to retreat.

CORELL. They shouldn't have sent a man like you here!

LANSER. Don't worry—as long as we can hold, we will hold. [*Crossing to* CORELL, *sadly.*] I can act quite apart from my knowledge. I will shoot the Mayor. [*His voice grows hard.*] I will not break the rules. I will shoot the doctor, I will help tear and burn the world. I don't like you, Corell. I am licking my wounds surely. And—I am giving you wounds to lick. [*Crosses around to front of table R. end.*] Sergeant!

SERGEANT. [*Enters U.L., crosses D.L.C.*] Sir?

LANSER. [*Slowly.*] Place Mayor Orden and Dr. Winter under arrest!

[SERGEANT *turns, exits.* LANSER *crosses to doors U.L. and exits.* CORELL *looks after them, then turns back to table, looks at it, places his hands on it, then slowly seats himself in the chair* LANSER *vacated.*]

CURTAIN

PART TWO

Scene IV

Time: *About half an hour later.*
Scene: *The same as before.*
At Rise: *The table has been cleaned up. One* soldier *stands to the R. of doors U.L.* mayor *is standing at the R. window looking out.*

mayor. [*Crossing to table.*] Where is Colonel Lanser? [*The* soldier *does not answer.*] Please tell Colonel Lanser I wish to see him. [mayor *turns and crosses R. As he does* winter *enters U.L. followed by a* soldier. mayor *turns to them.*] Doctor.

winter. [*Crossing to chair L. end table.*] Well, Your Excellency. This is one time you didn't send for me. I guess we're being held as hostages.

mayor. [*Crossing to him.*] Well, we've been together in everything else. I suppose it was bound to come. They're afraid of us now. I'm glad it's come.

winter. They think that because they have only one leader and one head that we are like that. They know that ten heads lopped off would destroy them. [*Crosses to chair L. of table, sits.*] But we are a free people. We have as many heads as we have people. Leaders pop up like mushrooms in a time of need.

mayor. [*Crossing L. to chair, patting* winter's *shoulder as he passes above him.*] Thank you. I knew it, but it is good to hear you say it. The people won't go under, will they?

winter. No. They'll grow stronger with outside help.

95

MAYOR. [*Sits chair L.C.*] I can talk to you, Doctor. I'm thinking of my own death. If they follow the usual course, they must kill me, and then they must kill you. [WINTER *is silent*.] Mustn't they?

WINTER. I guess so.

MAYOR. You know so. [*He is silent a moment*] I am a little man in a little town. But there must be a spark in little men that can burst into flame. At first I was afraid. I thought of all the things I might do to save my own life. And then that went away and now I feel a kind of exaltation, as though I were bigger and better than I am. It's like—well, do you remember in school, a long time ago, I delivered Socrates' denunciation? I was exalted then, too.

WINTER. You were indeed.

MAYOR. I was Socrates. I denounced the school board. I bellowed at them. And I could see their faces grow red.

WINTER. They were holding their breaths to keep from laughing. I remember well. It was graduation and your shirt tail was sticking out.

MAYOR. [*Raises his head, looks at the ceiling.*] Um— Um— Um— How did it go?

WINTER. Let me see—it begins— [*Prompting him.*] "And now, Oh men."

MAYOR. [*Softly.*] "And now, oh men who have condemned me—
I would fain prophesy to you—
For I am about to die—"

[LANSER *comes quietly into the room, crosses above table to R. end and stops on hearing the word.* MAYOR *looks at the ceiling, lost in trying to remember.*]

"And—in the hour of death—
Men are gifted with prophetic power.

And I—prophesy to you, who are my murderers,
That immediately after my—
my death—"
WINTER. [*Breaking in.*] Departure.
MAYOR. What?
WINTER. The word is departure, not death. You made the
same mistake before.
MAYOR. No. It's death. [LANSER *puts his helmet on table.*
MAYOR *looks around and sees* LANSER *watching him.*]
Isn't it death?
LANSER. "Departure. Immediately after my departure."
WINTER. You see. That's two against one. Departure is
the word.
MAYOR. [*Looking straight ahead. His eyes in memory.
Seeing nothing outward.*]
"I prophesy to you who are my murderers,
That immediately after my departure,
Punishment far heavier than you have inflicted upon me
Will surely await you.
Me you have killed because you wanted to escape the
     accuser
And not to give an account of your lives . . ."
[*Softly.*] "But that will not be as you suppose—far
     otherwise."
[*His voice grows stronger.*] "For I say that there will
     be more accusers of you than there are now,
Accusers whom hitherto I have restrained.
If you think that by killing men, you can prevent some-
     one from censoring your lives—you are mistaken."
[*He thinks for a time, smiles embarrassedly.*] That's all
     I can remember.
WINTER. It's very good after forty-six years.
LANSER. Mayor Orden, I have arrested you as a hostage.
For the good behavior of your people. These are my
orders.

MAYOR. [*Simply.*] You don't understand. When I become a hindrance to the people, they'll do without me.

LANSER. [*Crossing R. to armchair.*] The people know you will be shot if they light another fuse. [*Turns to him.*] Will they light it?

MAYOR. They will light the fuse.

LANSER. Suppose you ask them not to?

MAYOR. [*Looks at him, slowly.*] I am not a very brave man, sir. I think they will light it anyway. I hope they will. But if I ask them not to, they will be sorry.

LANSER. But they will light it?

MAYOR. Yes, they will light it. I have no choice of living or dying, you see, sir. But—I do have a choice of how I do it. If I tell them not to fight, they will be sorry. But they will fight. If I tell them to fight, they will be glad. And I, who am not a very brave man, will have made them a little braver. [*He smiles apologetically.*] It's an easy thing to do, since the end for me is the same.

LANSER. [*Crossing to armchair R.*] If you say yes, we will tell them you said no. [WINTER *rises.*] We will tell them you begged for your life. [*Sits.*]

WINTER. [*Angrily, crossing to* LANSER.] They would know. You don't keep secrets. One of your men got out of hand one night and he said the flies had conquered the fly-paper. Now the whole nation knows his words. They have made a song of it. You do not keep secrets. [*Crosses U.R. to table.*]

LANSER. Mayor Orden, I think a proclamation from you might save many lives.

MAYOR. [*Quietly.*] Nothing can change it. You will be destroyed and driven out.

MADAME. [*Enters U.L., crosses to* MAYOR.] What is this all about?

[LANSER *rises.*]

MAYOR. Be quiet a moment, dear. [*His voice is very soft.*]
The people don't like to be conquered, sir. And so they
will not be. Free men cannot start a war. But once it is
started, they can fight on in defeat. Herd men, followers
of a leader, they cannot do that. And so it is always that
herd men win battles, but free men win wars. You will
find it is so, sir.

LANSER. [*Crosses to R. end table.*] My orders are clear.
[*Looks at watch.*] Eleven o'clock is the dead-line. I have
taken my hostages. If there is violence I will execute
them.

WINTER. [*Crosses D. to R. of* LANSER.] And you will
carry out the orders, knowing they will fail.

[*From the distance there is the sound of an explosion.*
LANSER *looks at* WINTER. *They stand tensely listening
and a second explosion comes.* LANSER *and* MAYOR *look
toward windows.*]

LANSER. I will carry out my orders.

MADAME. I wish you would tell me what all this nonsense is.

[LANSER *picks up his helmet from table.*]

MAYOR. [*Turns to her, takes her hand.*] It's nonsense,
dear.

MADAME. But they can't arrest the Mayor.

MAYOR. No, they can't arrest the Mayor. The Mayor is
an idea conceived by free men. [*To* LANSER.] It will escape arrest.

MADAME. You've forgotten it again. You always forget—
Wait here. I'll get it for you. [*Exits U.L.*]

LANSER. [*Crosses to L.C., puts on helmet, clicks heels,
bows.*] Your Excellency! [*Exits U.L.—front door is
heard to slam.*]

[MAYOR *turns to* WINTER, *they exchange glances,* WINTER *crosses to stove.*]

MAYOR. [*Calls.*] Annie. [*The door R. opens instantly.*] Listening?

ANNIE. Yes, sir. [*Crosses to him.*]

MAYOR. [*Smiles, takes her hands.*] Annie, stay with Madame as long as she needs you. Don't leave her alone. [*Kisses her on forehead.*]

ANNIE. I'll take care of her, Your Excellency. [*Turns away, exits R.*]

MAYOR. Doctor, how did it go about the flies?

DOCTOR. The flies have conquered the fly-paper.

MAYOR. [*Chuckling to himself.*] The flies have conquered the fly-paper.

MADAME. [*Enters U.L., carrying* MAYOR's *chain of office, crosses to him.*] You always forget it. [*Places chain around his neck.*]

MAYOR. [*Looks at her. Puts his arm about her shoulders. Uses the same tone as earlier. He knows what she is doing.*] My dear—my very dear. [*Kisses her on cheek.*]

MADAME. Annie and Joseph are up to something in the kitchen. [*She crosses to R.C.*] I'll just have to . . . [*She stops as though to recall something, then crosses back to* MAYOR, *kisses him on the mouth, straightens his hair, and starts again for the kitchen.*] I'll just have to see what they're up to. [*Exits R.*]

[PRACKLE *enters from U.L., comes to attention above table. The two* SOLDIERS *snap to attention and shoulder their bayoneted rifles.*]

MAYOR. [*Turns to look at the* SOLDIERS, *then takes out his watch, turns to* WINTER.] Eleven o'clock.

WINTER. A time-minded people. [*He crosses to* MAYOR *who takes his watch and chain and puts them in* WINTER's *hand, then clasps his hands. They look at each other a moment, then* MAYOR *turns and crosses L.C. There he stops and turns back to* WINTER.] "Crito, I owe a cock to Ascalaepius. Will you remember to pay the debt?"

WINTER. [*Crosses C. to table.*] "The debt shall be paid."

MAYOR. [*Chuckling.*] I remembered that one.

WINTER. [*Very softly.*] Yes. You remembered it.

MAYOR. The debt will be paid! [*He turns and walks slowly to the door as another explosion is heard, this time closer.*]

[PRACKLE *goes ahead of him. The* SOLDIERS *follow him out as the*]

CURTAIN
COMES DOWN SLOWLY

PROPERTIES

Ash tray
Watch for Dr. Winter
Watch for Mayor
Mantle ornament
Pipe
Submachine gun
Small card
Heavy gold chain
Double-barrelled shotgun
Sporting rifle
Silver cigarette box with cigarettes and safety matches
Several cups of coffee
Maps, microscope, rock and ore specimens
Various paper documents
Drawing board, triangle, paper drawing, pen, pencils, etc., and velvet-lined box for pen
Shaving brush
Field glasses
Side arm and other small military equipment for wearing
Gas mask bag
Brown canvas, tube, iron tripod base, metal rod
Folded rotogravure page with pictures of undraped girls
Nail
White bandage for Correll
Several newspapers
Small dagger (side arm for Lanser)